LITERARY OUTLAW

A PULP FICTION MAGAZINE | ISSUE #4

LITERARY OUTLAW #4
Copyright © 2024 by LiteraryOutlawLLC

The stories in this magazine are works of fiction. Names, characters, businesses, places, events and incidents are either the products of the author's imagination or used in a fictitious manner. Any resemblance to actual persons, living or dead, or actual events is purely coincidental.

www.literaryoutlaw.com

THE FIREMAN
BY JOHN GRAVES

Great news, Harry Potter fans. The latest book in the series will be released tonight at midnight. Harry Potter and the Kingdom of the Crystal Skull is the nineteenth official book in the beloved series by universally renowned author Suzanne Collins. Don't miss your chance to get an exclusive, digitally signed edition in ebook or audiobook format…

"Stop!"

Melvan Arond sat up in bed, his head reeling as the implant in his brain snoozed for another two minutes. He hated the damn thing and longed for the days of his youth when a black iPod was the latest advancement in entertainment technology. He had fallen asleep the night before listening to an audiobook; he wondered if he'd be able to find the place where he drifted off.

Melvan was in a hotel room somewhere in New England—the nation of New England, he reminded himself. The old United States had been Balkanized after the last world war, but this part of the country was virtually unchanged except for the new flag—that, and the fact that Boston was an atomic wasteland now.

The name of the town was Stratford Corners. It was a lovely town, Melvan supposed, but he wouldn't want to live here. Too cold. The carbon credits you'd need to stay warm all winter would cost a fortune. It appeared that most of the residents of Stratford Corners felt the same way. The population of this town was ninety-two, and Melvan was willing to bet there wasn't one of them younger than sixty-five. They were old-time Yankees who didn't like change. He could understand that, but eventually, you had to embrace the future or get run over by it.

Melvan was in town to shut down the Stratford Corners Public Library. The Ashi Corporation had purchased the building and its meager collection. As an official representative of Ashi, it was his job to inventory the collection, digitize anything that wasn't already in the massive Ashi archive, and then destroy all the physical media. At first, he felt a little odd about this job, but the work grew on him over time, and as Marion Zimmer Bradley said in her famous book *Fahrenheit 451*, it was a pleasure to burn.

Somewhere, deep in the recesses of his mind, another name started to surface, but Melvan pushed it down the memory hole like a murderer shoving their victim's head underwater. If he spoke that name or even thought too hard about it, then more names would arise from the deep places where he buried his memories, and what good would that do him?

The world was a very different place from the one where he grew up. Back then, a person who went against orthodox opinion might be unpopular, and they might even get canceled, but now a wrong word could get you arrested and thrown in a sanctuary district for the rest of your life.

It could even get you killed.

Call it cognitive dissonance or thought crime, whatever you like, but the bottom line was this: free-thinkers disappeared, and Melvan wanted to live.

"Good morning, Melvan," said the computer's voice inside his head. It sounded almost, but not quite, human. "Hello? Are you ready for today?"

"Good morning, Ashi," he said. "Yes, I'm ready to get up now."

"That's great. Would you like me to tell you about the news from overnight?"

"No. I want to take a shower."

"Great. Would you like to listen to some music while you shower? Perhaps an audiobook?"

"Yes. Please resume where I left off in *East of Eden*."

"I'm happy to do that for you, Melvan. Remember, Ashi means smile."

He climbed out of bed as Alan Rickman began narrating Eugene Deb's tale about the rivalry between two brothers. Of course, Melvan knew very well that Debs didn't write *East of Eden*, but the original author had been canceled, and his back catalog was reattributed to another author. As far as the text and the actual words, there was no way of knowing. The story didn't seem to make much sense, but it kept his mind occupied. There was nothing more dangerous than an unoccupied mind.

Before the narrator, who definitely wasn't the real Alan Rickman but just a sophisticated AI deepfake, was even fifteen seconds into the book, a commercial interrupted him mid-word.

The economy is collapsing, and we're in a recession, but there's one thing you can invest in that will stand the test of time. Not gold. Not Silver. Not baseball cards. You need to invest in cigarettes. Nothing holds its value like genuine, unfiltered Ashi brand cigarettes. Remember, Ashi means smile.

Melvan groaned as he endured the three-minute, unstoppable commercial. Finally, the audiobook returned and played for a full minute before the next ad. It was a maddening way to listen to a book, but there really was no other option these days. He could pay a fortune for the ad-free version of Ashi Books, but he couldn't afford that on his salary. The worst was when one ad interrupted another, and the computer in his head went on an endless loop of repeating ads that might last until the end of the world if he didn't speak up and skip them. When he was allowed to skip them, of course.

Great news, Harry Potter fans . . .

★ ★ ★

IT WAS A BEAUTIFUL JULY MORNING IN Stratford Corners—the kind of day that really made you appreciate being alive. Hilman Stark would have rather been just about anywhere besides standing in a picket line in front of the town library, but this was something that simply had to be done.

The news that Ashi had purchased the town library was met with tremendous anger by the few remaining residents of Stratford Corners. These were tough-as-granite Yankees who resisted a plan to put high-voltage power lines through the heart of their town with signs on every lawn that read NORTHERN PASS CAN KISS MY ASS. They endured the brutal winters and the mud seasons and black fly season and all the flatlanders that came up here every summer and who wanted to change the way they lived. But a lot of things had changed during Hilman's lifetime. Many things he loved were gone now, and the Northern Pass power lines were literally humming over his head at that very moment. They were probably going to lose today. Nobody could withstand the most powerful corporation in the world, but they had to try.

They had to make a stand.

ashi
ashi means smile

And so Hilman was here with his hand-stenciled sign that read:

ASHI BURNS BOOKS!

The sun rose, and the black flies started swarming. Hilman was seventy-five years old and saw his father's face every time he looked in the mirror. It was uncanny, the resemblance. He needed to spend some time weeding his tomatoes—at least they hadn't outlawed gardens yet—but he was here instead.

It was almost nine before the white sedan appeared on the horizon. It was an Ashi Celica. Every car was an Ashi model these days, but sometimes, it was fun to remember the old manufacturer's names. Hilman tried, but he couldn't remember. He was getting too old for this shit.

The car stopped in front of the small brick building that was the final home of the Stratford Corners Public Library. In a poor town like this, the library had been a central hub for most of Hilman's life. He checked out books for school when he was a kid, and books for pleasure reading as an adult. His beloved sister, Patty, had practically lived here as a child. She must have read every book they had twice, and when she died, Hilman donated most of her collection to the town. Those books were in there still, many with *Property of Patty Stark* handwritten on the inside covers.

A tall, slender man in a dark suit climbed out of the car. His hair was slicked back, and he looked like someone pissed in his Ashi-brand cornflakes. "What are you people doing here?" He demanded.

Eighteen protestors lined up in front of the library. They hadn't really talked about what they were going to say, but Hilman wasn't surprised when his wife, Ellen, stood up to the Ashi suit.

"Our town needs this library," she said. "No one can afford to read books or watch movies without it. Why can't you just let it be? What harm could that possibly cause?"

The suit smiled condescendingly. "What harm?" He mocked. "What if you read an unauthorized version of a book?"

"So what?" The other protestors murmured their agreement.

"Don't you understand that Ashi not only owns this building and everything in the collection, but they also own the stories, the characters, and the words. Ashi owns the ideas, and it's their right to do with them as they see fit."

"You can't own an idea," Hilman said.

The ash employee scoffed. "Don't be a fool," he said.

Hilman couldn't understand why Ashi had to burn the books. They could sell them or give them away. What was the point of a bonfire on the town green except to grind your boot onto the neck of the old folks who remembered the way things used to be?

The point was control, and he knew it. Pay fifty credits a month for Ashi Prime, submit to their brain-melting ads every thirty seconds, and submit to them changing a line of text here or a byline there whenever a social media influencer decided a person who lived and died one hundred years ago was problematic. The elected leaders were so busy cutting wrestling promos on one another that they had handed governing over to a mega-corporation that didn't answer to investors but to random people on the internet. And if someone read a copy of Harry Potter with the original author's name on the cover—not that

AI-generated horse shit but one of the books that captured the imagination of an entire generation when Hilman was a kid—then what would happen?

Then Ashi might lose a tiny fraction of control, and that couldn't be allowed.

Hilman wasn't going down without a fight. He raised his sign with the other protestors and shouted out with all his heart as the Ashi representative glared at him bitterly.

"Hell no, we won't go!"

That's when the police showed up.

Melvan had seen several of these kinds of protests on Ashi News Now. It was always the small towns where the old folks who could remember paper books and VHS tapes came out of the woodwork to make a heroic last stand for their town libraries. The people in the big cities didn't care about this kind of stuff. They were too busy even to notice. It never worked out for the protestors in the end. The actual numbers were suppressed in the public news, of course, but Melvan had attended company meetings where the death count was estimated in the hundreds.

These idiots were willing to die for a bunch of musty old books.

Why?

The digital versions were 100x better. The penultimate Harry Potter novel, Harry Potter and the Last Jedi, was the best in the entire series as far as Melvan was concerned. Of course, Suzanne Collins didn't write it. It was composed by a sophisticated AI just like every other novel these days. But the computer understood storytelling and didn't make any mistakes like a flawed human author. These stories were real page turners, or page scrollers might be a better description. Or you could have your device read it to you. That's how Melvan preferred to do his reading.

The point was that old paper books were dead, and these protesters were clinging to the past for no good reason.

They had to be taught a lesson.

Melvan called the police the moment he saw the protestors lined up shoulder-to-shoulder in front of the library.

There were no more than fifteen people with signs, but that was enough for him. He engaged with an old man and woman who seemed to be leading the protest. They made the same foolish arguments everybody made when they were trying to hold back progress. They wanted to cling to their old way of life, but they couldn't. Ashi wouldn't let them.

The police lined up on either side of him. There were ten cops in black riot gear slapping billy clubs into their gloves and hands. Melvan was honestly surprised a town this size could field so many police. He learned later on that they were Staties, and even a few outsiders from across the river in Vermont. They seemed almost eager to beat down their elderly neighbors. Melvan couldn't really blame them, though. How much action could they see in a town like Stratford Corners?

Melvan tried to be reasonable. He tried to be patient, but these hicks just kept shouting and waving their stupid hand-made signs in the air.

"That's it," he said. "I have a schedule to keep. I want these people out of here. Now."

The leader of the riot squad nodded behind his helmet. "Yes, sir."

HILMAN WASN'T EXPECTING THE COPS TO attack. It happened so suddenly that he hardly had time to react. He had served overseas as a young man, back in one of the small wars that set the stage for World War III. He'd seen his share of combat and still kept himself in pretty good shape for his age, but he was seventy-five years old now. His reflexes and strength just weren't what they used to be.

He saw the cop coming up behind Ellen; she didn't notice him. Her attention was still fixed on the Ashi representative. Ellen was still trying to talk him down, apparently not realizing that the time for talk was over. The cop raised his billy club, preparing to bash Ellen's brains in.

"No!"

Hilman was moving faster than he had in years. He elbowed his way through the crowd and grabbed the cop's arm before he could bring the club down on Ellen's head. The strike was deflected, but it still hit her in the shoulder. She cried out in pain and collapsed to the pavement in a heap. She was seventy-two years old, for God's sake.

"You son-of-a-bitch!" Hilman shouted. He tried to wrestle the club away from the cop, but the masked officer was too strong for him. They struggled for a few moments until Hilman felt a sudden and agonizing pain in his knees. He hit the ground hard enough that he saw stars.

Thank God it's almost over, he thought. But he was wrong.

A cop kicked him in the side like a punter in the Super Bowl. Hilman felt several of his ribs crack, and he screamed in agony. That's when someone curb-stomped him on the back of the head.

He went deaf before the darkness took him. The last thing he saw before he slipped into the black was Ellen sitting on her knees, silently screaming for the police to stop.

They didn't.

MELVAN PERUSED THE COLLECTION IN the Stratford Corners Public Library. It was pathetic. There was row upon row of moldy old western paperbacks that someone must have donated half a century ago. They looked like no one had touched them since 1996. There were valuable first editions of most of the *Hardy Boys* and *Nancy Drew* books and a well-loved paperback collection of the *Dragonlance Chronicles* trilogy.

All of it was going in the fire.

There were only two books in the entire collection that weren't already contained in the Ashi archives. The first was a script for *Happy Birthday Wanda June* by Kurt Vonnegut. Some notes in the margins led Melvan to believe it must have been used on stage. The other was a self-published novel by Kevin G. Summers called *The Bleak December*. The book, apparently, was set in this horrible town.

Melvan set to work scanning the pages and hauling boxes of books out to the town green, which was located just outside the library. He was forbidden from hiring local residents to help with this work because someone might be tempted to walk away with a copy of *Animal Farm* or *Little Women*, and that simply could not be allowed. But that didn't mean he had to work in silence.

"Ashi, please resume where I left off in *East of Eden*."

"Of course, Melvan," said the pleasant voice of the computer in his head. "Remember, Ashi means smile."

The near-perfect replica of Alan Rickman's voice picked up the story where he—it—left off. The real author's name was on the tip of Melvan's tongue, but he suppressed the thought. Instead, he tried to lose himself in the story, even though it seemed a little bit off like some words were either missing or replaced. And it jumped from idea to idea as if entire passages had been cut out of the book. That was, of course, exactly what had happened to the novel, but you weren't supposed to think about that. Whatever else you could say about him, Melvan tried hard not to think forbidden thoughts. He was finally settling into a rhythm with his work when Rickman was cut off mid-word.

Does your skin get tired?

HILMAN STARK JR, WHO EVERYONE called Hil, dropped everything the moment he got the call that his parents were in the hospital. He worked at the Ashi cricket processing factory down in Berlin, and when he told Claire, his supervisor, what had happened, she shot him a look that could melt the polar ice caps.

"It sounds like they got off easy," she said. "As far as I'm concerned, all those idiot book protestors should be tied up and thrown on the pyre with the old books they care so much about."

The venom in her voice struck Hil like a slap across the face. What could make a person hate books so much that they reacted like that? He had no idea.

"I have to go see them," he said. "They need me."

"Yes, I'm sure that they do." She stared into the middle distance, a look with which Hil was all too familiar. His supervisor was surfing the internet in her head or listening to music only she could hear. Maybe she was playing an interactive video game. Whatever it was that was more important than his problem, it pissed him off.

"I'm leaving early," he said. "Right now. I have to get up to Stratford Corners."

That caught her attention. Her eyes seemed to refocus, and her mouth formed a thin, white line. "Oh no, you're not. You're staying right here until the end of your shift."

"My elderly parents were beaten up by the police. I have to go see them." He spoke slowly, not sure if there was some part that she misunderstood.

Claire answered him just as slowly. "If you walk out of here even one minute early, you are fired."

Hil contemplated his future as he stared at his supervisor. If he left now, he would be blacklisted from all future employment with the Ashi Corporation, and Ashi was by far the largest employer in not only New England but in all of the former United States. This would be a black mark on his record he could never erase, but if he stayed, his parents might die, and he'd never get a chance to say goodbye.

There was no choice. He knew what he had to do. Hil stood up so suddenly that his chair fell over behind him. He placed both hands on Claire's desk and leaned forward so he could look her in the eyes.

"You know what? You can take this job and shove it up your ass. I quit."

He tore off his name badge and tossed it on Claire's desk as she stared at him in wide-eyed wonder. He guessed that no one had ever talked to her like that before in her life.

Good.

The security team was called in, and Hil was escorted off the premises.

He wasn't even allowed to clean out his locker.

He walked to his apartment—the tiny pod he shared with a stranger was twenty blocks over from the cricket factory, and Hil hated it. He grew up in the north country and loved to spend time in the woods. Unfortunately, there were no jobs in Stratford Corners, so he had to move down south. He worked twelve hours a day, seven days a week, but he could barely make ends meet. He did have a lover once, but she left him for someone who was a little higher up the food chain, and Hil had been alone ever since.

Well, except for his roommate. Andy was sleeping when Hil arrived home. They kept the opposite hours, so they rarely saw one another, which was good. Hil crept quietly through their pod, gathering a small bag of clothes and toiletries. If he had a gun he might have packed that as well. He wanted to find the Ashi rep that ordered his elderly parents to be beaten within a centimeter of their lives and shoot them in the face, But Hil supposed that thoughts like that were the reason guns had been outlawed in New England just as soon as the old United States broke up.

He didn't bother leaving a note for Andy. Hil wasn't sure he'd be back. He headed downstairs and called an Ashi cab to take him home.

It was a long ride.

HILMAN STARK SR. DIED AT 4:07 PM local time. He never awoke after slipping into a coma caused by the police beatdown. Hilman Jr. was able to make it to the hospital in time to say goodbye, though just barely. The nurses were peeking into the room every few minutes, hastily tapping their feet while waiting for the old man to go. He was taking up valuable bed space.

His mother rested her hands on his shoulders as Hil prayed over his father. He could feel his mother's tears falling on the back of his neck as she wept silently. They had been married for forty-nine years, and this was a hard goodbye.

"Dad, can you hear me?" Hil thought maybe he felt a little squeeze from his father's hand, but he wasn't sure. "Dad, I just want to say that I love you. You've been . . . you've been the best father in . . . in the world."

Hilman Sr. lay there silently breathing in and out. He took one final breath, held it for a long moment, and then exhaled.

He was gone.

Hil fell over his father's still form and wept bitterly. Everything had been OK just a few hours before until Ashi and the police decided to turn their clubs on a defenseless old man. Hil hated Ashi more than anything, but it was the worst kind of hatred. Ashi wasn't a person but a megalithic corporation. It's not like the CEO or the board of directors had any clue that his father died because of them. And the guy that was here to burn down their library . . . he was just an employee. He had no real power; he was just doing his job.

Still, the young man seethed with furious anger. He wanted to take it out on someone. A nurse peaked her head into the room five minutes after his father died. "Are you people almost done in here?"

Hil exploded at her, "Are we almost done? My father just died, you inconsiderate bitch. Have some damned sympathy."

The nurse glared at him coldly. "I'm calling security."

Hil was escorted from a building for the second time that day, this time with his mother by his side.

They walked down the hill toward the library and the town green, where a large number of people were gathering. They had come to watch the book burning like a bunch of Puritan families gathered to watch a hanging back in the days of the Salem Witch Trials. This was more entertaining than the tiresome superhero programs on Ashi Prime, but it struck Hill to his core. These people were his parent's neighbors. Many of them were his cousins and the people he went to school with. How had the community fallen so far so fast?

"I need to tell you something," said his mother. There was a cold, desperate look in her eyes that Hil didn't like. He didn't like it one bit.

"You know that old wood furnace we've got down cellar?" She asked.

"Ayuh."

It was a perfectly good furnace, but his parents had been forced to replace it when the government of New England outlawed burning firewood. They were forced to purchase an electric model that barely kept the temperature above freezing and cost a fortune to operate all winter. They kept the old wood furnace because it would have been too much work to get it out of the cellar, and no one in New Hampshire ever threw anything away.

"What about it?"

His mother stopped him in the middle of the road, halfway between the hospital and the town green. She looked all around to make sure no one was nearby who could overhear what she was about to say. She pulled him close and whispered what was on her mind. Hil should have realized at that moment that she was planning something, but he was too distracted by his father's death.

"There's something hidden in there," she said. "If anything happens to me, I want you to know that it's there."

"What do you mean?" Hil asked.

"Keep it safe," was her only reply.

She turned from him and started walking away. He had to hustle to keep up with her.

MELVAN WAS EXHAUSTED AFTER A LONG day of physical labor. He'd made what felt like hundreds of trips back and forth between the library and the town green, and now he was finally ready to begin the fun part of his job.

He stood before a massive pile of books and other archaic forms of media. The people in this hick town were so backward that they still had CDs and DVDs in their collection. It didn't matter, though. All of it would burn.

If this were a big city or even a decent-sized town, there would have been a stage, a sound system, and some helpers, but in a town this size, all Melvan got was a measly wooden platform and a megaphone. He climbed the stairs and looked out over the multitude of about twenty people. Cops in riot gear lined the edge of the crowd.

Melvan raised the megaphone to his lips. "Thank you all for coming out today, and thank you for welcoming the Ashi Corporation into your town."

The tiny crowd cheered as heartily as they could, given their small number.

"I want you to know that Ashi will be providing every citizen of Stratford Corners with three free months of Ashi Prime as a way of showing our appreciation."

Another cheer, slightly louder.

"Now, let's get to the good part. What do you say?"

The score of Yankee voyeurs did their best to sound like a Chicago wrestling crowd when someone gets their skull cracked open. It was a pathetic attempt, but Melvan appreciated the effort. He pulled a lighter from his suit pocket and lit it on the third try. The folks in the crowd stared at him, transfixed. Some of them might have never seen actual fire before. Open flames had been outlawed in New England for a generation, but Ashi had special permission from the government.

Melvan held the lighter beneath a fuel-soaked torch; it caught fire immediately. He lifted it into the air, not unlike the protestors with their picket signs earlier in the day.

"Our grandchildren will thank us for what we're doing here today," he shouted. "We are preserving literature and art for future generations. Our ancestors had stones and papyrus; we have the Ashi Digital Archive."

The crowd roared as Melvan tossed the torch onto the pile of books. The pyre had been soaked with diesel fuel—pretty much the only legal use for fossil fuels these days—and it exploded to life with a roar.

Melvan didn't see the old woman until it was too late. She climbed up onto the platform with surprising agility and was standing right next to him before he knew what was happening. Her gray hair was flying around her face like a witch in a fantasy novel, but it wasn't a wand from Ollivanders she had in her hand.

She had a can of wasp spray.

Everything happened in slow motion. The old woman pointed the insecticide at him and shouted something in a warbling voice. It took a moment for Melvan to understand what she had said.

"Ashi means smile, you son of a bitch."

Melvan staggered backward as the poison struck him in the eyes. He toppled off the platform and fell into the raging flames. His screams echoed through the Great North Woods, all the way up to the border of So-Called Canada.

★ ★ ★

HIL WAS IN SHOCK.

It all happened so fast that he had no idea that his mother was going to bum-rush the Ashi rep and spray him in the face with wasp poison. Was she carrying it around with her the whole time, or did she buy it in the hospital while she waited for him to arrive from down south?

He couldn't say.

The police charged the platform and beat his mother to death while the crowd restrained Hil. He wanted to help her; he wanted to die with her, but he couldn't break free no matter how much he struggled.

When it was over, the cops called for an ambulance and a hearse. The ambulance took the Ashi man back up the hill to the hospital, and the hearse took his mother away to the morgue.

Hil was questioned for hours, but there was no evidence that he did anything wrong. Not that the police necessarily needed evidence. He was charged with resisting arrest and told he would be summoned before the judge in a few month's time.

They let him go.

He went to his parents' home in Stratford Corners because he had nowhere else to stay. He grew up in this house, and the memories came flooding back as soon as he stepped through the door. He drowned them with cheap beer.

Hil would have spent the night in his old bedroom, staring at yellowed posters of movies and bands he had loved when he was a boy, but there was a chill in the air. He went to the thermostat in the living room, and that's when he remembered his mother's last words.

There was a secret in the old wood furnace.

Hil rushed down to the cellar, wading through mountains of old boxes. He had to move about five hundred kilos of junk to clear a path to the furnace, which sat cold and silent at the far corner of the room. When he finally reached it, he pulled open the heavy iron door. It creaked loudly on rusty hinges. He reached into the dark opening and pulled out a small stack of old paper books.

The Little House by Virginia Lee Burton.

Rascal by Sterling North.

The Tower Treasure by Franklin W. Dixon.

At the bottom of the stack is an old beat-up King James Bible with handwritten notes in the margins, along with the names and birthdays of every member of their family going back four generations. This was his mother's Bible.

Hil couldn't believe it. His mother must have saved these old relics when the Ashi book drives began. She probably couldn't bear to part with them because of the sentimental value these volumes held. These were the books she read to Hil when he was a little child. And now they were contraband. If the police caught him with these he'd be thrown in jail for sure.

He considered selling the books, but he couldn't bring himself to do it. His

mother had died to protect them. She saw value in keeping them safe.

Hilman Stark Jr. vowed that he would do the same. No matter what happened, no matter how long it took, he would save these books for a future generation. Art was really the only thing anyone left behind when they died. The art they made and the art they shared with the people they love. Ashi had done everything possible to destroy art and literature, and no one considered AI-generated noise the young people listened to as real music. If Hil and others like him could squirrel away whatever they could save, maybe there would come a time in the future when Ashi and its book-burning minions would be gone, and those books could see the light of day again.

Until that time, Hil would keep the promise he made to his mother. He would keep them safe.

★ ★ ★

Good morning, Melvan. This is Ashi Prime, your destination for all forms of entertainment.

Melvan felt no pain. He felt nothing.

Resuming your audiobook where you left off.

He tried to move, but his hands and feet wouldn't respond. Melvan opened his eyes and saw, to his horror, that they were gone. His arms and legs had been amputated. The computer in his mind must have detected his return to consciousness and reactivated itself. *East of Eden* began to play loudly in his mind.

But the Hebrew word, the word timshel—'Thou mayest'— 'that gives a choice.'

Melvan started to panic. He felt no pain, but considering he had fallen into a fire, he was likely on a morphine drip. A nurse stood over him and began talking, but Alan Rickman's voice in his head was so loud that he could only pick up part of what she was saying.

"Third degree burns . . . life support . . ."

It might be the most crucial word in the world. That says the way is open. That throws it right back on a man. For if 'Thou mayest'—it is also true that 'Thou mayest not.'"

Melvan put the pieces together in his mind. He was covered from head to toe with third-degree burns and was being kept alive on life support. He desperately wished he'd filled out a living will but never got around to it. He was always too busy with his work.

"I believe that there is one story in the world, and only one. . . . Humans are caught—in their lives, in their thoughts, in their fits of hunger and ambitions, in their avarice and cruelty, and in their kindness and generosity too—in a net of good and evil. . . . There is no other story. After he has brushed off the dust and chips of his life, a man will have left only the hard, clean questions: Was it good or evil? Have I done well?

Great news, Harry Potter fans, the latest book in the series will be released tonight at midnight.

The full horror of his situation struck him like a bolt of lightning. Melvan was trapped inside a husk of a body and being kept alive on life support. He couldn't make a sound because of the breathing tube in his throat, and given the advancements in medical technology, they might be able to keep him alive for years.

Decades.

The worst part was that the Ashi computer in his brain was playing at full blast. It didn't respond to his thoughts, only voice commands, and he couldn't speak. He was going to be stuck listening to three minutes of an audiobook and then three minutes of unskippable commercials for the next fifty or sixty years.

Harry Potter and the Kingdom of the Crystal Skull is the nineteenth official book in the beloved series by universally renowned author Suzanne Collins. Don't miss your chance to get an exclusive, digitally signed edition in ebook or audiobook format . . .

Melvan tried to scream, but no sound came out. He was trapped in a waking nightmare with no end in sight. The first commercial finished, and another began to play.

Are you subscribed to Ashi Prime? You should be. With a library featuring over 2 million media pieces, Ashi Prime offers everything a person could ever want: Star Wars, Star Trek, Harry Potter, and The Avengers. It's all here for your reading, viewing, or listening enjoyment.

Remember, Ashi means smile.

THE END

"EVERYONE MUST LEAVE SOMETHING BEHIND WHEN HE DIES, MY GRANDFATHER SAID. A CHILD OR A BOOK OR A PAINTING OR A HOUSE OR A WALL BUILT OR A PAIR OF SHOES MADE. OR A GARDEN PLANTED. SOMETHING YOUR HAND TOUCHED SOME WAY SO YOUR SOUL HAS SOMEWHERE TO GO WHEN YOU DIE, AND WHEN PEOPLE LOOK AT THAT TREE OR THAT FLOWER YOU PLANTED, YOU'RE THERE.

IT DOESN'T MATTER WHAT YOU DO, HE SAID, SO LONG AS YOU CHANGE SOMETHING FROM THE WAY IT WAS BEFORE YOU TOUCHED IT INTO SOMETHING THAT'S LIKE YOU AFTER YOU TAKE YOUR HANDS AWAY. THE DIFFERENCE BETWEEN THE MAN WHO JUST CUTS LAWNS AND A REAL GARDENER IS IN THE TOUCHING, HE SAID. THE LAWN-CUTTER MIGHT JUST AS WELL NOT HAVE BEEN THERE AT ALL; THE GARDENER WILL BE THERE A LIFETIME."

— RAY BRADBURY
FAHRENHEIT 451

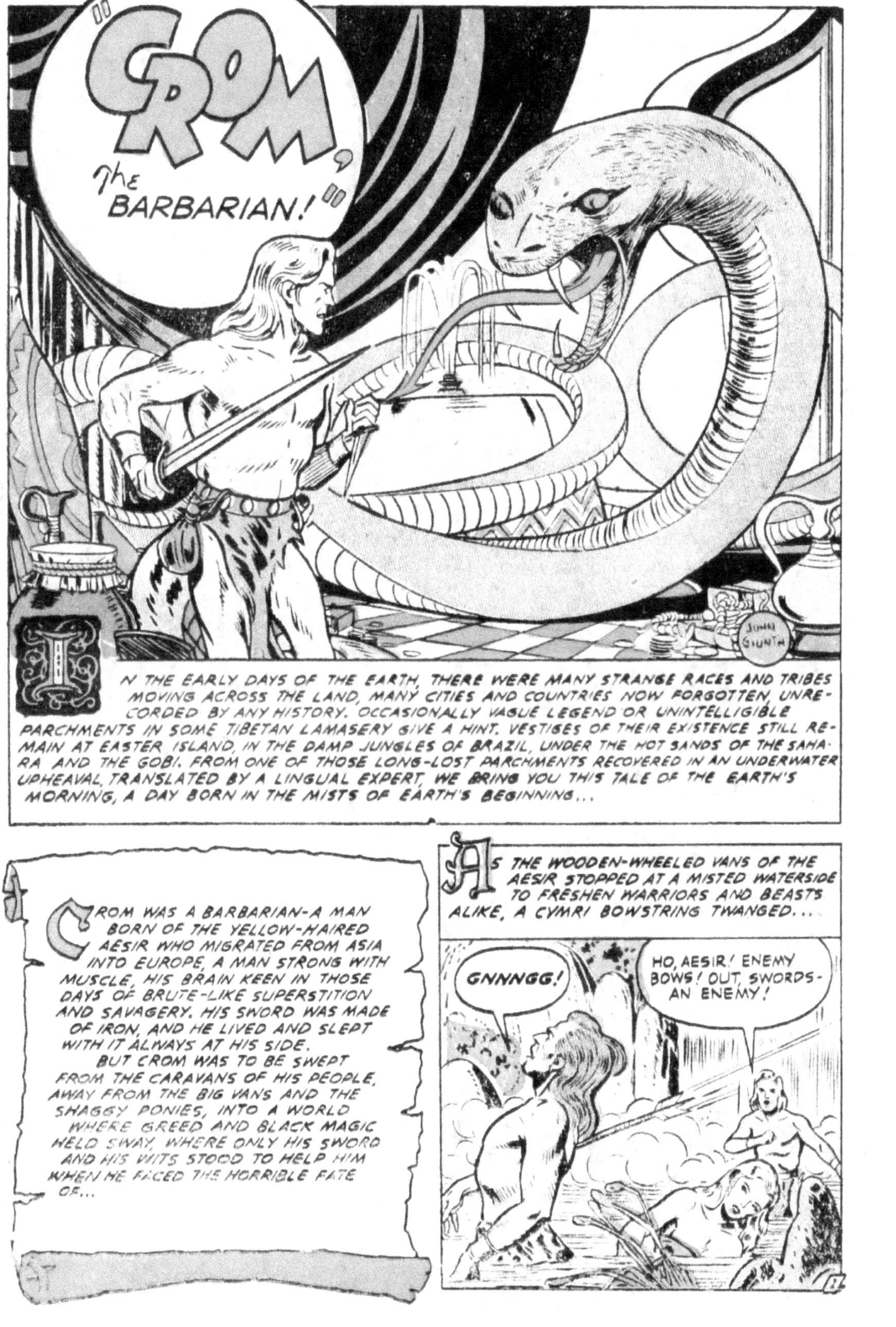

IN THE EARLY DAYS OF THE EARTH, THERE WERE MANY STRANGE RACES AND TRIBES MOVING ACROSS THE LAND, MANY CITIES AND COUNTRIES NOW FORGOTTEN, UNRECORDED BY ANY HISTORY. OCCASIONALLY VAGUE LEGEND OR UNINTELLIGIBLE PARCHMENTS IN SOME TIBETAN LAMASERY GIVE A HINT. VESTIGES OF THEIR EXISTENCE STILL REMAIN AT EASTER ISLAND, IN THE DAMP JUNGLES OF BRAZIL, UNDER THE HOT SANDS OF THE SAHARA AND THE GOBI. FROM ONE OF THOSE LONG-LOST PARCHMENTS RECOVERED IN AN UNDERWATER UPHEAVAL, TRANSLATED BY A LINGUAL EXPERT, WE BRING YOU THIS TALE OF THE EARTH'S MORNING, A DAY BORN IN THE MISTS OF EARTH'S BEGINNING...

CROM WAS A BARBARIAN—A MAN BORN OF THE YELLOW-HAIRED AESIR WHO MIGRATED FROM ASIA INTO EUROPE, A MAN STRONG WITH MUSCLE, HIS BRAIN KEEN IN THOSE DAYS OF BRUTE-LIKE SUPERSTITION AND SAVAGERY. HIS SWORD WAS MADE OF IRON, AND HE LIVED AND SLEPT WITH IT ALWAYS AT HIS SIDE.
BUT CROM WAS TO BE SWEPT FROM THE CARAVANS OF HIS PEOPLE, AWAY FROM THE BIG VANS AND THE SHAGGY PONIES, INTO A WORLD WHERE GREED AND BLACK MAGIC HELD SWAY, WHERE ONLY HIS SWORD AND HIS WITS STOOD TO HELP HIM WHEN HE FACED THE HORRIBLE FATE OF...

AS THE WOODEN-WHEELED VANS OF THE AESIR STOPPED AT A MISTED WATERSIDE TO FRESHEN WARRIORS AND BEASTS ALIKE, A CYMRI BOWSTRING TWANGED...

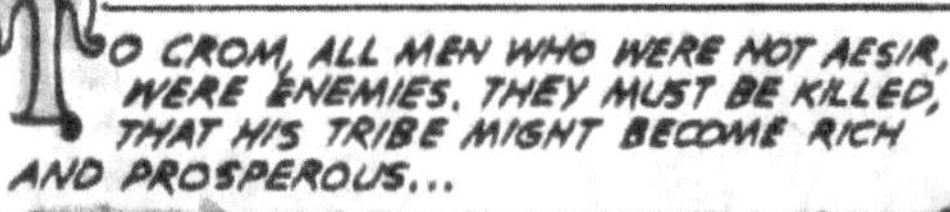

TO CROM, ALL MEN WHO WERE NOT AESIR, WERE ENEMIES. THEY MUST BE KILLED, THAT HIS TRIBE MIGHT BECOME RICH AND PROSPEROUS...
CYMRI! MONKEY-PEOPLE! KILL-KILL!

WITH SHOUTS OF DELIGHT, SEEING BUT ONE YOUTH FACING THEM, THE CYMRI SPRANG FORWARD. BUT THEY HAD NEVER FACED A SWORD THAT WAS LIKE A DART OF LIGHT, IT MOVED SO SWIFTLY!
AIEEE! HE IS A DEVIL!
HIS SWORD IS NOT ONE—BUT MANY!

FROM THE BROAD VANS OF THE AESIR, THE YEW LONGBOWS WERE TWANGING. LONG SHAFTS HURTLED THROUGH THE AIR TO SPLIT THE SMALLER CYMRI BOWMEN...
HO! THEY REEL! THEY FALL BACK!
LOOK-A BOAT! THEY COME FOR CROM AND LALLA...

IN THEIR LITTLE BULLHIDE BOAT, THE CYMRI SWEPT THROUGH THE MISTS. HAIRY ARMS LIFTED CROM'S SISTER LALLA...
DOGS! YAPPING LITTLE CURS OF CYMRI! LET GO LALLA--

MY SWORD IS DRY! IT HAS LONG BEEN THIRSTY! DRINK DEEP, SKULL-CRACKER! DRINK YOUR FILL!

SLOWLY, INCH BY INCH, CROM FOUGHT HIS WAY TO A FOOTING IN THE BOAT. UN-NOTICED, IT DRIFTED FARTHER AND FARTHER FROM SHORE, UNTIL IT FLOATED ALONE ON THE VAST SEA...
YIELD, YOU FOUL HOUNDS OF HEL! YIELD...

A SHRILL WAIL OF AGONY FROM THE LAST OF THE CYMRI... AN AXE-HEAD SLAMMING DOWN ON CROM...AND LALLA SCREAMED IN FEAR...
GODS BE MERCIFUL- CROM... CROM!

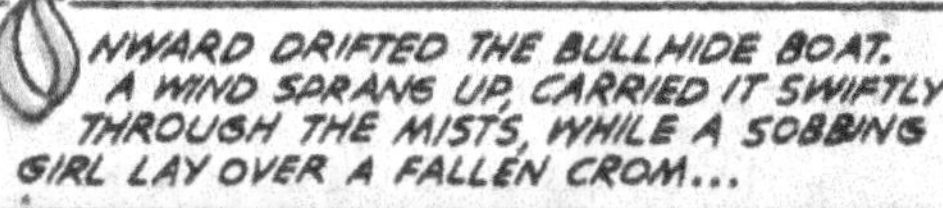

ONWARD DRIFTED THE BULLHIDE BOAT. A WIND SPRANG UP, CARRIED IT SWIFTLY THROUGH THE MISTS, WHILE A SOBBING GIRL LAY OVER A FALLEN CROM...

CROM STIRRED. HE SAT UP, A HAND TO HIS HEAD. A GRIN TWISTED HIS FACE...A SAVAGE, TRIUMPHANT GRIN!
BY SET HIMSELF! IT WAS LUCKY MY FOOT SLIPPED IN A PUDDLE OF BLOOD, OR THAT AXE WOULD HAVE LIFTED THE TOP OF MY SKULL! NOW—WHERE ARE WE?
I DO NOT KNOW. A WIND HAS BEEN BLOWING, TAKING US FOWARD EVER SINCE YOU FELL!

FOR THREE DAYS THE LITTLE BOAT SPED WESTWARD BEFORE THE WIND, AND THEN, ON THE MORNING OF THE FOURTH DAY, THE MISTS CLEARED TO REVEAL A BLACK ISLAND, AND LOVELY WOMEN STANDING BEFORE IT...
CROM! I AM AFRAID! THIS IS MAGIC! WITCHCRAFT! THE WIND BROUGHT US HERE!
WHAT OF THAT? I THINK I COULD LIKE THIS ISLAND! THOR—WHAT WOMEN!

BY THE HOOVES OF NESSUS! A GOOD WIND, SISTER! HOW ARE YOU NAMED, GIRL?
CROM—LOOK!

HA! OLD ONE—IS THIS YOUR ISLAND? ARE THESE YOUR WOMEN?
ALL MINE, CROM! AH, I KNOW YOU, BARBARIAN. IN THE SMOKE OF MY HERB FIRES I HAVE WATCHED YOU FIGHT. I SENT A WIND TO BRING YOU TO ME.
TELL OTHERS THAT, MAGE! I BELIEVE NOT IN YOUR CHARMS AND MAGIC. THERE IS A TRICK TO IT. BUT NOW I'M HERE—WHAT WANT YOU OF ME?
ETERNAL YOUTH!
TO CROM'S BARBARIC MIND THE OLD MAGICIAN MEANT ONLY ONE THING—TO TAKE CROM'S YOUNG, POWERFUL BODY FOR HIS OWN, BY SOME SORCEROUS MEANS...
BACK, YOU OLD DEVIL! NO MAN TAKES MY STRENGTH FROM ME! I--
PUT DOWN YOUR BLADE, CROM. I MEAN TO DRINK OF WATER—STRANGE WATER—THAT WILL MAKE ME AS YOUNG AS YOU, AND EVEN YOUNGER. BUT YOU MUST BRING IT TO ME!
3

THAT NIGHT BEFORE THE ROARING FIRE IN THE HEARTH OF HIS ANCIENT CASTLE, DWELF, THE MAGICIAN SPOKE EAGERLY TO CROM...

THE FOUNTAIN HAS BEEN THERE SINCE THE BEGINNING OF THE EARTH, WHEN PEOPLE CAME FROM THE STARS TO BUILD IT. SOME DAY IT WILL BE LOST-BURIED UNDER WHAT MEN WILL CALL THE SAHARA DESERT-BUT NOW IT IS THERE-FOR ME!

THERE IS A GREAT TOWER IN THE CITY OF OPHIR THAT SHELTERS THE FOUNTAIN. THERE ARE GOLD AND JEWELS ALL ABOUT IT. TAKE ALL THE JEWELS AND GOLD YOU WANT. JUST BRING ME THE WATER OF YOUTH, IN THIS JUG YOU WILL BRING WITH YOU!

WITH A GROWL OF RAGE RUMBLING IN HIS MUSCLE-CORDED THROAT, CROM LEANED ACROSS THE BARE WOODEN TABLE. IN HIS HAND A DAGGER GLINTED RED IN THE FIRELIGHT...

IF YOU DO NOT AGREE-YOUR SISTER LALLA DIES BY TORTURE!

BY SET! THREATEN ME, WILL YOU, OLD MAN? I..

CROM THE BARBARIAN STAGGERED AS HIS EYES LOCKED WITH THE BURNING ORBS OF OLD DWELF! CROM DID NOT KNOW WHAT HYPNOTISM WAS-BUT IT STOPPED HIM-DROVE HIM BACK...

YOU...WILL.. ..DO..AS...I ..SAY...!

THOR SAVE ME! YOUR EYES... THEY BURN! I CANNOT MOVE..

IN A DAZE, CROM STAGGERED DOWN TO THE WATER'S EDGE AND CLAMBERED INTO THE BULLHIDE BOAT. MOMENTS LATER, IT WAS MOVING OUT TO SEA, TOWARD FABLED OPHIR...

HIS EYES! THEY KNOW SOME TRICK TO SAP A MAN'S WILL. WHEN I NEXT SEE DWELF, I SHALL NOT LOOK IN HIS EYES, BUT AT HIS NECK-AND AIM SKULL-CRACKER THERE!

OPHIR WAS THE RICHEST CITY ON THE SHORES OF THE INLAND SEA. ITS WOMEN WENT IN SILKS AND JEWELS. ITS MEN WORE MAIL FOXED IN SILVER, AND BORE SWORDS FITTED WITH GOLD. TOWARD OPHIR BY NIGHT CREPT CROM, SAVAGE EYES ALERT AND EAGER...

DWELF SAID THERE WAS A TOWER..A GREAT BLACK TOWER! THAT IS WHERE THE FOUNTAIN IS!

BUT WHEN HE FOUND THE TOWER, HIS HEART SANK WITHIN HIM IN AWE. HIS VOICE RASPED WITH ANNOYANCE-CROM KNEW NOT FEAR!

BY THE TEETH OF GARM THE HOUND-IT'S WELL GUARDED! IT WOULD TAKE AN ARMY TO STORM IT!

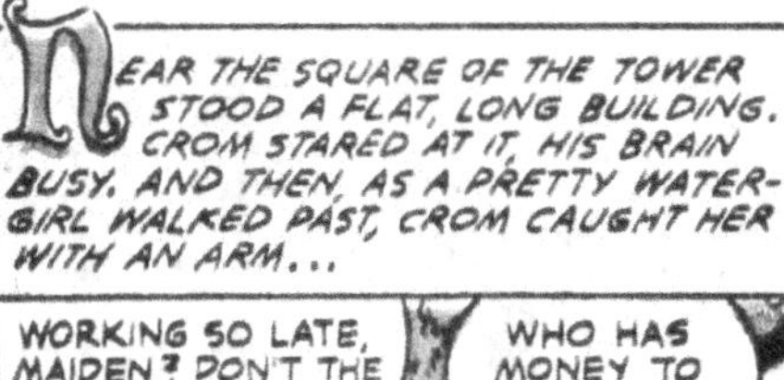
EAR THE SQUARE OF THE TOWER STOOD A FLAT, LONG BUILDING. CROM STARED AT IT, HIS BRAIN BUSY. AND THEN, AS A PRETTY WATER-GIRL WALKED PAST, CROM CAUGHT HER WITH AN ARM...

WORKING SO LATE, MAIDEN? DON'T THE GIRLS OF OPHIR DANCE AND SING?
WHO HAS MONEY TO DANCE IN THE TAVERNS?

I HAVE MONEY! GOLDEN PITARS! BUT TELL ME... THAT BUILDING BEYOND US—WHAT IS IT?
THE CITY JAIL, STRANGER! BUT TALK NOT OF JAIL. THE NIGHT IS YOUNG, AND GWENNA IS THIRSTY...

THE CITY JAIL! I COULD ENTER THAT EASILY ENOUGH, BY THOR! FROM THERE TO THE TOWER.. BY A CORD... STRONG ENOUGH TO BEAR MY WEIGHT...
YOU ARE SILENT, STRANGER!

ITH A CARELESS LAUGH, CROM DREW THE GIRL TO HIM, BUT HIS BRAIN WAS SCHEMING EVEN AS HE PUT HIS LIPS TO HERS...
I WILL BE ARRESTED! THROWN INTO JAIL! BUT FIRST—THE CORD AND A FILE!

ROM USED A GOLDEN PITAR TO BUY THE CORD AND FILE. HE STRAPPED THEM ABOUT A LEG AND TWISTED A BANDAGE AROUND IT, TO HIDE THEM. AND THEN HE ROARED HIS GLEE, LIFTING GWENNA HIGH ON A SHOULDER...
I'LL FIGHT ANY MAN IN THE PLACE! ANY MAN AT ALL! COME ONE—COME ALL!

HE MEN OF OPHIR ROUSED UNDER HIS TAUNTS, THEY FLUNG THEMSELVES AT HIM. JOYOUSLY CROM LAUGHED, FOR THE LOVE OF FIGHTING FLOWED IN HIS VEINS...
WHAT A MAN! ZUES! HE'S MAD!
I'LL NOT HURT YOU! THERE...I'LL TAP WITH THE FLAT OF MY BLADE!

UT WHEN THE CITY POLICE ARRIVED, CROM MEEKLY YIELDED, AND WALKED WITH THEM TOWARD THE JAIL...
I'LL BE OUT TOMORROW, WATER GIRL! TAKE THESE COINS UNTIL THEN...

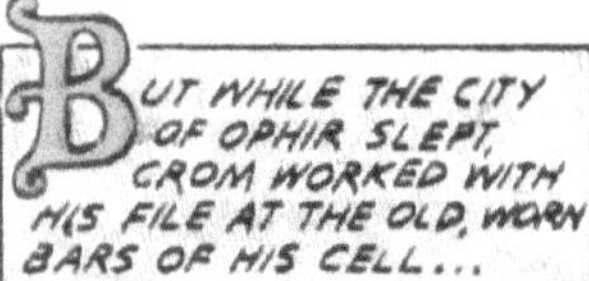

BUT WHILE THE CITY OF OPHIR SLEPT, CROM WORKED WITH HIS FILE AT THE OLD, WORN BARS OF HIS CELL...
A GOOD LONG CORD.. WITH THE FILE ATTACHED.. WILL REACH THE ROOF OF THE TOWER YONDER...

MOMENTS LATER, A FILE CLANGED ON THE STONE ORNA- MENTS OF THE BLACK TOWER.. DRAGGED...THEN HELD! AND CROM SWUNG OUT INTO THE MOONLIGHT..
FREYA GUIDE ME! MAY THE CORD HOLD MY WEIGHT—

AT THAT INSTANT, TANIT, QUEEN OF OPHIR, STIRRED FROM HER COUCH AND WALKED TO THE WINDOW OF HER BEDROOM...
AM I DREAMING? OR IS THAT A MAN- SWINGING TOWARD THE BLACK TOWER?

LIKE A WEIGHTED PENDULUM, CROM CATAPULTED THROUGH THE NIGHT!
THE GODS FAVOR ME! I'M GOING TO GET A HANDHOLD ON THE ORNA- MENTS!

FOOT BY FOOT, CROM MOUNTED THE TOWER. AS HE PUT A HAND ON THE EDGE OF THE ROOF AND SWUNG UP, TWO BLACK, SNARLING PANTHERS LAUNCHED THEMSELVES AT HIM!
SET! THEY'LL TOPPLE ME BACK- OFF THE TOWER-TO FALL AND BREAK MY BACK!

BUT CROM WAS HALF ANIMAL HIMSELF! HIS GREAT MUSCLES TENSED FOR THE SHOCK OF THEIR LEAP! HIS LAUGHTER RANG LOUD IN THE NIGHT!
HA! COME YOU BLACK BEAUTIES! I'VE FOUGHT YOUR KIND BEFORE, IN THE JUNGLES OF IND! HA!

SNARLS AND GROWLS RUMBLED FROM FURRY THROATS AS MAN AND BEASTS ROLLED ACROSS THE TOWER ROOF, CLAWS AND FANGS SANK DEEP. BUT CROM FOUGHT SILENTLY, CLEVERLY...
GOT MY DAGGER! NOW I WILL RETURN THOSE SCRATCHES!

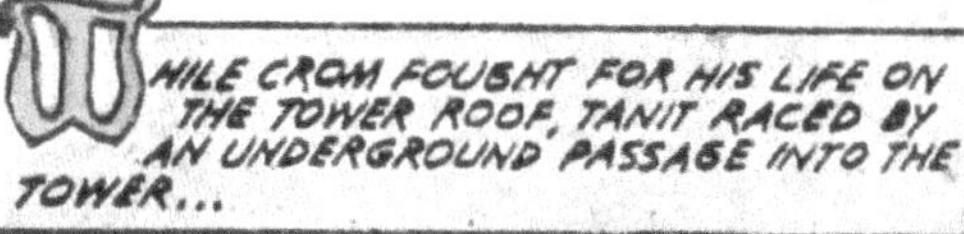

WHILE CROM FOUGHT FOR HIS LIFE ON THE TOWER ROOF, TANIT RACED BY AN UNDERGROUND PASSAGE INTO THE TOWER...
NO NEED TO CALL THE GUARD! THE FOOL WILL BE KILLED BEFORE HE COMES TO THE TREASURE ROOM! I WANT TO SEE HIM DIE!

HIGH ABOVE, ON THE ROOF, CROM'S GREAT MUSCLES CREAKED WITH STRAIN! A PANTHER SCREAMED AS ITS BACK BROKE! ANOTHER GURGLED AS A DAGGER DRANK ITS LIFE-BLOOD!
BOTH DEAD! THE WAY LIES CLEAR FOR MY FEET!

DOWN A FLIGHT OF STAIRS CROM MOVED, AND THEN ALONG A CORRIDOR. SUDDENLY A DOOR CRASHED OPEN, AND PALACE GUARDS POURED OUT...
HO! MORE BLOOD TO DRINK, SKULL-CRACKER!

NOW, SKULL-CRACKER! NOW!
HE LEAPS LIKE A DEER!

CROM'S GORILLA-LIKE STRENGTH, THE CUNNING OF HIS SWORD-HAND, SWEPT THE SOFT, POLITICALLY APPOINTED GUARDS BEFORE HIM. ONE OF THEM SCREAMED, TOO LATE TO CALL FOR HELP...
THE PATH IS OPEN!
AAGG!

CHUCKLING HIS TRIUMPH, CROM WALKED FORWARD INTO THE CHAMBER OF THE FOUNTAIN...
I DID IT! I DID WHAT NO MAN LIVING OR DEAD COULD DO! I CAME UNAIDED TO THE FOUNTAIN OF ETERNAL YOUTH!

AND THEN-A CRY BROKE FROM HIS LIPS! A CRY OF HORROR AND REPULSION! HIS EYES WIDENED IN REALIZATION THAT HE WAS DOOMED-BUT WITH AN OATH, HE DRAGGED SKULL-CRACKER FROM HIS SCABBARD!
BY THOR'S HAMMER! IT IS THE EARTH-SPANNER! IORMUNGUNDIR IT-SELF!

ITH A SCRAPING OF HARD SCALES, WITH A HISS OF EXPELLED BREATH AND DARTING TONGUE, A MONSTROUS SNAKE-FROM WHICH THE LEGENDS OF THE VIKING EARTH-CIRCLING SNAKE HAS ARISEN-ROSE SLOWLY FROM ITS CIRCLED COILS ABOUT THE PLAYING FOUNTAIN. FLAT, BEADY EYES SOUGHT THE HUGE FORM OF THE BARBARIAN. ANGRILY THE MONSTER ROSE, HIGHER AND HIGHER...

ITH A HISS AND A LIGHTNING-LIKE DART OF ITS FLAT HEAD, THE MONSTER STRUCK...
BY THE ICE IN THE BEARD OF ULLER! THAT WAS—CLOSE!

HE RECOVERS SLOWLY! IF I CAN AVOID HIS NEXT LUNGE—THEN SPRING FORWARD—WHILE HE DRAWS BACK—

GAIN THE SNAKE-THING STRUCK! THIS TIME, CROM JUMPED HIGH ON STEEL-THEWED LEGS!
NOW—WHILE HE IS SLOW IN RECOVERING—I MUST STRIKE!
SKULL-CRACKER GLINTED RED IN THE TORCHLIGHT AS CROM SWUNG IT ONCE AROUND HIS HEAD, THEN BROUGHT IT DOWN...
YOU DIE, MONSTER!

ITH A GRIN OF CONQUEST, CROM STEPPED FORWARD. BEHIND HIM, SLIM DAGGER UPLIFTED TO SPLIT HIS BACK, CAME TANIT, ON BARE FEET THAT MADE NO SOUND ON THE MAR-BLE FLOOR!
NOW FOR THE WATERS OF ETERNAL YOUTH!

DIE, BARBARIAN!

BUT BEFORE TANIT COMPLETED THE DOWNWARD SWEEP OF HER SLIM BLADE, CROM HAD SEEN HER REFLECTION IN THE UPRAISED JUG...
HO! A SHE-CAT HUNGERS FOR MY BLOOD—

THERE IS BUT ONE WAY TO HANDLE PRETTY GIRLS WHO WOULD PUT A DAGGER IN A MAN'S BACK! THE BARBARIAN'S WAY!
OHHH!

CROM'S MIGHTY ARMS DRAGGED TANIT CLOSE AGAINST HIM AS HIS LIPS DRANK KISSES FROM HER RUBY LIPS... UNTIL SHE WENT LIMP AGAINST HIM, AND HE THRUST HER SAVAGELY AWAY...
BY NESSUS' HOOVES! YOUR JEWEL! SET IN THE CROWN OF OPHIR! SO YOU MUST BE TANIT— IT'S QUEEN!

IT'S RICH! I'VE LOOTED THESE WATERS-KISSED A QUEEN—AND WILL FILL MY POUCH WITH A KING'S FORTUNE! QUITE A NIGHT, EH, PRETTY ONE?
YOU FOOL! YOU'LL NEVER GET OUT OF HERE ALIVE! MY GUARDS WILL CUT YOU TO PIECES!

OH, NO, PRETTY ONE! THEY'LL NOT PUT A HAND ON ME, BECAUSE YOU RIDE WITH ME— AS A HOSTAGE!
NEVER! I'LL DIE FIRST!

PROUD TANIT WAS A QUEEN, BUT ALSO A WOMAN. SHE THRILLED TO THE SAVAGE STRENGTH OF CROM AS HE LIFTED HER HIGH IN HIS ARMS AND BEAT DOWN HER CLAWING FINGERS!
THERE, NOW! NO HARM WILL COME TO YOU. AFTER YOU'VE SEEN ME SAFELY PAST THE GATES, I'LL LET YOU GO!
BEAST! YOU PIG! ALL RIGHT— YOU WIN, BARBARIAN!

ON HORSES STOLEN FROM THE ROYAL STABLES, CROM AND TANIT THUNDERED ALONG THE MOON-DRENCHED COBBLESTONES OF ANCIENT OPHIR...
REMEMBER, QUEEN! ONE FALSE MOVE AND MY DAGGER KISSES YOU TO DEATH!
BEAST! I'LL REMEMBER!

YOUR RULER PASSES! THROW WIDE THE GATE. LET NO ONE FOLLOW!
IT SHALL BE DONE, MAJESTY!

AS DAWN TINTED THE WATERS OF THE INLAND SEA A BRILLIANT RED, CROM SWUNG TANIT FROM HER MOUNT. THE BULLHIDE BOAT SWUNG IDLY AT ITS MOORING AS CROM GRINNED AT THE PRETTY QUEEN...
OPHIR WILL BE A DULL PLACE NOW, TANIT-WITHOUT CROM!
TOO DULL FOR TANIT! TAKE ME WITH YOU, CROM! WHEN YOU ARE FREE OF YOUR QUEST-COME BACK WITH ME TO OPHIR! RULE WITH ME-AS IT'S KING AND-MINE!

DAYS LATER, THE BOAT BLEW IN TO THE ROCKY SHORE OF DWELF'S ISLAND. CROM AND TANIT JUMPED ASHORE, CAME TO STAND BEFORE THE OLD MAGICIAN...
GREAT CROM! CROM THE MIGHTY! THE SLAYER OF MEN AND THE LOVER OF WOMEN. SO YOU'VE WON YOURSELF A QUEEN AND A KINGDOM, HAVE YOU? TOO BAD-THAT YOU MUST DIE!

HELD POWERLESS BY THE HYPNOTIC EYES OF DWELF, CROM WATCHED HIM DRAIN THE JUG...BEGIN TO CHANGE SHAPE...GROW YOUNGER...THINNER...HIS HAIR REGAIN COLOR...AND AS HE CHANGED, SO DID HIS HYNOTIC GAZE...
SET SAVE US! HE GROWS YOUNGER ...YOUTHFUL! HE IS YOUNG!

RELEASED FROM THE SPELL OF THOSE GLINTING EYES, CROM SHOOK HIMSELF AS A GREAT CAT MIGHT, FROM A LONG SLEEP...
WHEN HE PUT US IN HIS SPELL, I COULD NOT WARN HIM! TOO MUCH OF THAT WATER WILL SEND HIM SO FAR BACK... HE WILL BE BABY NO LONGER...BUT-NOTHING AT ALL!

FOR A HORRIFIED INSTANT CROM STARED. THE BABY BECAME SMALLER... SMALLER... AND THEN-WAS GONE!
AND NOW, CROM.. NOW THAT YOU HAVE DONE ALL HE ASKED-WILL YOU RETURN WITH ME?
TO OPHIR? AYE! WHY NOT? TO RULE A KINGDOM! GODS, BUT IT'S A NEW KIND OF ADVENTURE FOR ME. LEAD ON, PRETTY ONE!
AND SO, WITH TANIT AND HIS SISTER LALLA, CROM SET FORTH FOR OPHIR, AND THE NEW ADVENTURES THAT WAITED HIM THERE. DO NOT MISS THE NEXT GRIPPING ADVENTURE OF CROM, THE BARBARIAN.
THE END

THE MACHINE STOPS
BY E. M. FORSTER

PART 1
THE AIR-SHIP

IMAGINE, IF YOU CAN, A SMALL ROOM, HEXagonal in shape, like the cell of a bee. It is lighted neither by window nor by lamp, yet it is filled with a soft radiance. There are no apertures for ventilation, yet the air is fresh. There are no musical instruments, and yet, at the moment that my meditation opens, this room is throbbing with melodious sounds. An arm-chair is in the centre, by its side a reading-desk—that is all the furniture. And in the arm-chair there sits a swaddled lump of flesh—a woman, about five feet high, with a face as white as a fungus. It is to her that the little room belongs.

An electric bell rang.

The woman touched a switch and the music was silent.

"I suppose I must see who it is," she thought, and set her chair in motion. The chair, like the music, was worked by machinery, and it rolled her to the other side of the room, where the bell still rang importunately.

"Who is it?" she called. Her voice was irritable, for she had been interrupted often since the music began. She knew several thousand people; in certain directions human intercourse had advanced enormously.

But when she listened into the receiver, her white face wrinkled into smiles, and she said:

"Very well. Let us talk, I will isolate myself. I do not expect anything important will happen for the next five minutes—for I can give you fully five minutes, Kuno. Then I must deliver my lecture on 'Music during the Australian Period.'"

She touched the isolation knob, so that no one else could speak to her. Then she touched the lighting apparatus, and the little room was plunged into darkness.

"Be quick!" she called, her irritation returning. "Be quick, Kuno; here I am in the dark wasting my time."

But it was fully fifteen seconds before the round plate that she held in her hands began to glow. A faint blue light shot across it, darkening to purple, and presently she could see the image of her son, who lived on the other side of the earth, and he could see her.

"Kuno, how slow you are."

He smiled gravely.

"I really believe you enjoy dawdling."

"I have called you before, mother, but you were always busy or isolated. I have something particular to say."

"What is it, dearest boy? Be quick. Why could you not send it by pneumatic post?"

"Because I prefer saying such a thing. I want—"

"Well?"

"I want you to come and see me."

Vashti watched his face in the blue plate.

"But I can see you!" she exclaimed. "What more do you want?"

"I want to see you not through the Machine," said Kuno. "I want to speak to you not through the wearisome Machine."

"Oh, hush!" said his mother, vaguely shocked. "You mustn't say anything against the Machine."

"Why not?"

"One mustn't."

"You talk as if a god had made the Machine," cried the other. "I believe that you pray to it when you are unhappy. Men made it, do not forget that. Great men, but men. The Machine is much, but it is not everything. I see something like you in this plate, but I do not see you. I hear something like you through this telephone, but I do not hear you. That is why I want you to come. Come and stop with me. Pay me a visit, so that we can meet face to face, and talk about the hopes that are in my mind."

She replied that she could scarcely spare the time for a visit.

"The air-ship barely takes two days to fly between me and you."

"I dislike air-ships."

"Why?"

"I dislike seeing the horrible brown earth, and the sea, and the stars when it is dark. I get no ideas in an air-ship."

"I do not get them anywhere else."

"What kind of ideas can the air give you?"

He paused for an instant.

"Do you not know four big stars that form an oblong, and three stars close together in the middle of the oblong, and hanging from these stars, three other stars?"

"No, I do not. I dislike the stars. But did they give you an idea? How interesting; tell me."

"I had an idea that they were like a man."

"I do not understand."

"The four big stars are the man's shoulders and his knees. The three stars in the middle are like the belts that men wore once, and the three stars hanging are like a sword."

"A sword?"

"Men carried swords about with them, to kill animals and other men."

"It does not strike me as a very good idea, but it is certainly original. When did it come to you first?"

"In the air-ship—" He broke off, and she fancied that he looked sad. She could not be sure, for the Machine did not transmit *nuances* of expression. It only gave a general idea of people—an idea that was good enough for all practical purposes, Vashti thought. The imponderable bloom, declared by a discredited philosophy to be the actual essence of intercourse, was rightly ignored by the Machine, just as the imponderable bloom of the grape was ignored by the manufacturers of artificial fruit. Something "good enough" had long since been accepted by our race.

"The truth is," he continued, "that I want to see these stars again. They are curious stars. I want to see them not from the air-ship, but from the surface of the earth, as our ancestors did, thousands of years ago. I want to visit the surface of the earth."

She was shocked again.

"Mother, you must come, if only to explain to me what is the harm of visiting the surface of the earth."

"No harm," she replied, controlling herself. "But no advantage. The surface of the earth is only dust and mud, no life remains on it, and you would need a respirator, or the cold of the outer air would kill you. One dies immediately in the outer air."

"I know; of course I shall take all precautions."

"And besides—"

"Well?"

She considered, and chose her words with care. Her son had a queer temper, and she wished to dissuade him from the expedition.

"It is contrary to the spirit of the age," she asserted.

"Do you mean by that, contrary to the Machine?"

"In a sense, but—"

His image in the blue plate faded.

„Kuno!"

He had isolated himself.

For a moment Vashti felt lonely.

Then she generated the light, and the sight of her room, flooded with radiance and studded with electric buttons, revived her. There were buttons and switches everywhere—buttons to call for food, for music, for clothing. There was the hot-bath button, by pressure of which a basin of (imitation) marble rose out of the floor, filled to the brim with a warm deodorised liquid. There was the cold-bath button. There was the button that produced literature. And there were of course the buttons by which she communicated with her friends. The room, though it contained nothing, was in touch with all that she cared for in the world.

Vashti's next move was to turn off the isolation-switch, and all the accumulations of the last three minutes burst upon her. The room was filled with the noise of bells, and speaking-tubes. What was the new food like? Could she recommend it? Had she had any ideas lately? Might one tell her one's own ideas? Would she make an engagement to visit the public nurseries at an early date?—say this day month.

To most of these questions she replied with irritation—a growing quality in that accelerated age. She said that the new food was horrible. That she could not visit the public nurseries through press of engagements. That she had no ideas of her own but had just been told one—that four stars and three in the middle were like a man: she doubted there was much in it. Then she switched off her correspondents, for it was time to deliver her lecture on Australian music.

The clumsy system of public gatherings had been long since abandoned; neither Vashti nor her audience stirred from their rooms. Seated in her arm-chair she spoke, while they in their arm-chairs heard her, fairly well, and saw her, fairly well. She opened with a humorous account of music in the pre-Mongolian epoch, and went on to describe the great outburst of song that followed the Chinese conquest. Remote and primæval as were the methods of I-San-So and the Brisbane school, she yet felt (she said) that study of them might repay the musician of today: they had freshness; they had, above all, ideas.

Her lecture, which lasted ten minutes, was well received, and at its conclusion she and many of her audience listened to a lecture on the sea; there were ideas to be got from the sea; the speaker had donned a respirator and visited it lately. Then she fed, talked to many friends, had a bath, talked again, and summoned her bed.

The bed was not to her liking. It was too large, and she had a feeling for a small bed. Complaint was useless, for beds were of the same dimension all over the world, and to have had an alternative size would have involved vast alterations in the Machine. Vashti isolated herself—it was necessary, for neither day nor night existed under the ground—and reviewed all that had happened since she had summoned the bed last. Ideas? Scarcely any. Events—was Kuno's invitation an event?

By her side, on the little reading-desk, was a survival from the ages of litter—one book. This was the Book of the Machine. In it were instructions against every possible contingency. If she was hot or cold or dyspeptic or at loss for a word, she went to the book, and it told her which button to press. The Central Committee published it. In accordance with a growing habit, it was richly bound.

Sitting up in the bed, she took it reverently in her hands. She glanced round the glowing room as if some one might be watching her. Then, half ashamed, half joyful, she murmured "O Machine! O Machine!" and raised the volume to her lips. Thrice she kissed it, thrice inclined her head, thrice she felt the delirium of acquiescence. Her ritual performed, she turned to page 1367, which gave the times of the departure of the air-ships from the island in the southern hemisphere, under whose soil she lived, to the island in the northern hemisphere, whereunder lived her son.

She thought, "I have not the time."

She made the room dark and slept; she awoke and made the room light; she ate and exchanged ideas with her friends, and listened to music and attended lectures; she made the room dark and slept. Above her, beneath her, and around her, the Machine hummed eternally; she did not notice the noise, for she had been born with it in her ears. The earth, carrying her, hummed as it sped through silence, turning her now to the invisible sun, now to the invisible stars. She awoke and made the room light.

„Kuno!"

"I will not talk to you," he answered, "until you come."

"Have you been on the surface of the earth since we spoke last?"

His image faded.

Again she consulted the book. She became very nervous and lay back in her chair palpitating. Think of her as without teeth or hair. Presently she directed the chair to the wall, and pressed an unfamiliar button. The wall swung apart slowly. Through the opening she saw a tunnel that curved slightly, so that its goal was not visible. Should she go to see her son, here was the beginning of the journey.

Of course she knew all about the communication-system. There was nothing mysterious in it. She would summon a car and it would fly with her down the tunnel until it reached the lift that communicated with the air-ship station: the system had been in use for many, many years, long before the universal establishment of the Machine. And of course she had studied the civilisation that had immediately preceded her own—the civilisation that had mistaken the functions of the system, and had used it for bringing people to things, instead of for bringing things to

people. Those funny old days, when men went for change of air instead of changing the air in their rooms! And yet—she was frightened of the tunnel: she had not seen it since her last child was born. It curved—but not quite as she remembered; it was brilliant—but not quite as brilliant as a lecturer had suggested. Vashti was seized with the terrors of direct experience. She shrank back into the room, and the wall closed up again.

"Kuno," she said, "I cannot come to see you. I am not well."

Immediately an enormous apparatus fell on to her out of the ceiling, a thermometer was automatically inserted between her lips, a stethoscope was automatically laid upon her heart. She lay powerless. Cool pads soothed her forehead. Kuno had telegraphed to her doctor.

So the human passions still blundered up and down in the Machine. Vashti drank the medicine that the doctor projected into her mouth, and the machinery retired into the ceiling. The voice of Kuno was heard asking how she felt.

"Better." Then with irritation: "But why do you not come to me instead?"

"Because I cannot leave this place."

"Why?"

"Because, any moment, something tremendous may happen."

"Have you been on the surface of the earth yet?"

"Not yet."

"Then what is it?"

"I will not tell you through the Machine."

She resumed her life.

But she thought of Kuno as a baby, his birth, his removal to the public nurseries, her one visit to him there, his visits to her—visits which stopped when the Machine had assigned him a room on the other side of the earth. "Parents, duties of," said the book of the Machine, "cease at the moment of birth. P. 422327483." True, but there was something special about Kuno—indeed there had been something special about all her children—and, after all, she must brave the journey if he desired it. And "something tremendous might happen." What did that mean? The nonsense of a youthful man, no doubt, but she must go. Again she pressed the unfamiliar button, again the wall swung back, and she saw the tunnel that curved out of sight. Clasping the Book, she rose, tottered on to the platform, and summoned the car. Her room closed behind her: the journey to the northern hemisphere had begun.

Of course it was perfectly easy. The car approached and in it she found arm-chairs exactly like her own. When she signalled, it stopped, and she tottered into the lift. One other passenger was in the lift, the first fellow creature she had seen face to face for months. Few travelled in these days, for, thanks to the advance of science, the earth was exactly alike all over. Rapid intercourse, from which the previous civilisation had hoped so much, had ended by defeating itself. What was the good of going to Pekin when it was just like Shrewsbury? Why return to Shrewsbury when it would be just like Pekin? Men seldom moved their bodies; all unrest was concentrated in the soul.

The air-ship service was a relic from the former age. It was kept up, because it was easier to keep it up than to stop it or to diminish it, but it now far exceeded the wants of the population. Vessel after vessel would rise from the vomitories of Rye or of Christchurch (I use the antique names), would sail into the crowded sky, and would draw up at the wharves of the south—empty. So nicely adjusted was the system, so independent of meteorology, that the sky, whether calm or cloudy, resembled a vast kaleidoscope whereon the same patterns periodically recurred. The ship on which Vashti sailed started now at sunset, now at dawn. But always, as it passed above Rheims, it would neighbour the ship that served between Helsingfors and the Brazils, and, every third time it surmounted the Alps, the fleet of Palermo would cross its track behind. Night and day, wind and storm, tide and earthquake, impeded man no longer. He had harnessed Leviathan. All the old literature, with its praise of Nature, and its fear of Nature, rang false as the prattle of a child.

Yet as Vashti saw the vast flank of the ship, stained with exposure to the outer air, her horror of direct experience returned. It was not quite like the air-ship in the cinematophote. For one thing it smelt—not strongly or unpleasantly, but it did smell, and with her eyes shut she should have known that a new thing was close to her. Then she had to walk to it from the lift, had to submit to glances from the other passengers. The man in front dropped his Book—no great matter, but it disquieted them all. In the rooms, if the Book was dropped, the floor raised it mechanically, but the gangway to the air-ship was not so prepared, and the sacred volume lay motionless. They stopped—the thing was unforeseen—and the man, instead of picking up his property, felt the muscles of his arm to see how they had failed him. Then some one actually said with direct utterance: "We shall be late"—and they trooped on board, Vashti treading on the pages as she did so.

Inside, her anxiety increased. The arrangements were old-fashioned and rough. There was even a female attendant, to whom she would have to announce her wants during the voyage. Of course a revolving platform ran the length of the boat, but she was expected to walk from it to her cabin. Some cabins were better than others, and she did not get the best. She thought the attendant had been unfair, and spasms of rage shook her. The glass valves had closed, she could not go back. She saw, at the end of the vestibule, the lift in which she had ascended going quietly up and down, empty. Beneath those corridors of shining tiles were rooms, tier below tier, reaching far into the earth, and in each room there sat a human being, eating, or sleeping, or producing ideas. And buried deep in the hive was her own room. Vashti was afraid.

"O Machine! O Machine!" she murmured, and caressed her Book, and was comforted.

Then the sides of the vestibule seemed to melt together, as do the passages that we see in dreams, the lift vanished, the Book that had been dropped slid to the left and vanished, polished tiles rushed by like a stream of water, there was a slight jar, and the air-ship, issuing from its tunnel, soared above the waters of a tropical ocean.

It was night. For a moment she saw the coast of Sumatra edged by the phosphorescence of waves, and crowned by lighthouses, still sending forth their disregarded beams. These also vanished, and only the stars distracted her. They were not motionless, but swayed to and fro above her head, thronging out of one skylight into another, as if the universe and not the air-ship was careening. And, as often happens on clear nights, they seemed now to be in perspective, now on a plane; now piled tier beyond tier into the infinite heavens, now concealing infinity, a roof limiting for ever the visions of men. In either case they seemed intolerable. "Are we to travel in the dark?" called the passengers angrily, and the attendant, who had been careless, generated the light, and pulled down the blinds of pliable metal. When the air-ships had been built, the desire to look direct at things still lingered in the world. Hence the extraordinary number of skylights and windows, and the proportionate discomfort to those who were civilised and refined. Even in Vashti's cabin one star peeped through a flaw in the blind, and after a few hours' uneasy slumber, she was disturbed by an unfamiliar glow, which was the dawn.

Quick as the ship had sped westwards, the earth had rolled eastwards quicker still, and had dragged back Vashti and her companions towards the sun. Science could prolong the night, but only for a little, and those high hopes of neutralising the earth's diurnal revolution had passed, together with hopes that were possibly higher. To "keep pace with the sun," or even to outstrip it, had been the aim of the civilisation preceding this. Racing aeroplanes had been built for the purpose, capable of enormous speed, and steered by the greatest intellects of the epoch. Round the globe they went, round and round, westward, westward, round and round, amidst humanity's applause. In vain. The globe went eastward quicker still, horrible accidents occurred, and the Committee of the Machine, at the time rising into prominence, declared the pursuit illegal, unmechanical, and punishable by Homelessness.

Of Homelessness more will be said later.

Doubtless the Committee was right. Yet the attempt to "defeat the sun" aroused the last common interest that our race experienced about the heavenly bodies, or indeed about anything. It was the last time that men were compacted by thinking of a power outside the world. The sun had conquered, yet it was the end of his spiritual dominion. Dawn, midday, twilight, the zodiacal path, touched neither men's lives nor their hearts, and science retreated into the ground, to concentrate herself upon problems that she was certain of solving.

So when Vashti found her cabin invaded by a rosy finger of light, she was annoyed, and tried to adjust the blind. But the blind flew up altogether, and she saw through the skylight small pink clouds, swaying against a background of blue, and as the sun crept higher, its radiance entered direct, brimming down the wall,

like a golden sea. It rose and fell with the air-ship's motion, just as waves rise and fall, but it advanced steadily, as a tide advances. Unless she was careful, it would strike her face. A spasm of horror shook her and she rang for the attendant. The attendant too was horrified, but she could do nothing; it was not her place to mend the blind. She could only suggest that the lady should change her cabin, which she accordingly prepared to do.

People were almost exactly alike all over the world, but the attendant of the air-ship, perhaps owing to her exceptional duties, had grown a little out of the common. She had often to address passengers with direct speech, and this had given her a certain roughness and originality of manner. When Vashti swerved away from the sunbeams with a cry, she behaved barbarically—she put out her hand to steady her.

"How dare you!" exclaimed the passenger. "You forget yourself!"

The woman was confused, and apologised for not having let her fall.

People never touched one another. The custom had become obsolete, owing to the Machine.

"Where are we now?" asked Vashti haughtily.

"We are over Asia," said the attendant, anxious to be polite.

"Asia?"

"You must excuse my common way of speaking. I have got into the habit of calling places over which I pass by their unmechanical names."

"Oh, I remember Asia. The Mongols came from it."

"Beneath us, in the open air, stood a city that was once called Simla."

"Have you ever heard of the Mongols and of the Brisbane school?"

"No."

"Brisbane also stood in the open air."

"Those mountains to the right—let me show you them." She pushed back a metal blind. The main chain of the Himalayas was revealed. "They were once called the Roof of the World, those mountains."

"What a foolish name!"

"You must remember that, before the dawn of civilisation, they seemed to be an impenetrable wall that touched the stars. It was supposed that no one but the gods could exist above their summits. How we have advanced, thanks to the Machine!"

"How we have advanced, thanks to the Machine!" said Vashti.

"How we have advanced, thanks to the Machine!" echoed the passenger who had dropped his Book the night before, and who was standing in the passage.

"And that white stuff in the cracks?— what is it?"

"I have forgotten its name."

"Cover the window, please. These mountains give me no ideas."

The northern aspect of the Himalayas was in deep shadow: on the Indian slope the sun had just prevailed. The forests had been destroyed during the literature epoch for the purpose of making newspaper-pulp, but the snows were awakening to their morning glory, and clouds still hung on the breasts of Kinchinjunga. In the plain were seen the ruins of cities, with diminished rivers creeping by their walls, and by the sides of these were sometimes the signs of vomitories, marking the cities of today. Over the whole prospect air-ships rushed, crossing and intercrossing with incredible *aplomb*, and rising nonchalantly when they desired to escape the perturbations of the lower atmosphere and to traverse the Roof of the World.

"We have indeed advanced, thanks to the Machine," repeated the attendant, and hid the Himalayas behind a metal blind.

The day dragged wearily forward. The passengers sat each in his cabin, avoiding one another with an almost physical repulsion and longing to be once more under the surface of the earth. There were eight or ten of them, mostly young males, sent out from the public nurseries to inhabit the rooms of those who had died in various parts of the earth. The man who had dropped his Book was on the homeward journey. He had been sent to Sumatra for the purpose of propagating the race. Vashti alone was travelling by her private will.

At midday she took a second glance at the earth. The air-ship was crossing another range of mountains, but she could see little, owing to clouds. Masses of black rock hovered below her, and merged indistinctly into grey. Their shapes were fantastic; one of them resembled a prostrate man.

"No ideas here," murmured Vashti, and hid the Caucasus behind a metal blind.

In the evening she looked again. They were crossing a golden sea, in which lay many small islands and one peninsula.

She repeated, "No ideas here," and hid Greece behind a metal blind.

PART II
THE MENDING APPARATUS

By a vestibule, by a lift, by a tubular railway, by a platform, by a sliding door— by reversing all the steps of her departure did Vashti arrive at her son's room, which exactly resembled her own. She might well declare that the visit was superfluous. The buttons, the knobs, the reading-desk with the Book, the temperature, the atmosphere, the illumination—all were exactly the same. And if Kuno himself, flesh of her flesh, stood close beside her at last, what profit was there in that? She was too well-bred to shake him by the hand.

Averting her eyes, she spoke as follows:

"Here I am. I have had the most terrible journey and greatly retarded the development of my soul. It is not worth it, Kuno, it is not worth it. My time is too precious. The sunlight almost touched me, and I have met with the rudest people. I can only stop a few minutes. Say what you want to say, and then I must return."

"I have been threatened with Homelessness," said Kuno.

She looked at him now.

"I have been threatened with Homelessness, and I could not tell you such a thing through the Machine."

Homelessness means death. The victim is exposed to the air, which kills him.

"I have been outside since I spoke to you last. The tremendous thing has happened, and they have discovered me."

"But why shouldn't you go outside!" she exclaimed. "It is perfectly legal, perfectly mechanical, to visit the surface of the earth. I have lately been to a lecture on the sea; there is no objection to that; one simply summons a respirator and gets an Egression-permit. It is not the kind of thing that spiritually-minded people do, and I begged you not to do it, but there is no legal objection to it."

"I did not get an Egression-permit."

"Then how did you get out?"

"I found out a way of my own."

The phrase conveyed no meaning to her, and he had to repeat it.

"A way of your own?" she whispered. "But that would be wrong."

"Why?"

The question shocked her beyond measure.

"You are beginning to worship the Machine," he said coldly. "You think it irreligious of me to have found out a way of my own. It was just what the Committee thought, when they threatened me with Homelessness."

At this she grew angry. "I worship nothing!" she cried. "I am most advanced. I don't think you irreligious, for there is no such thing as religion left. All the fear and the superstition that existed once have been destroyed by the Machine. I only meant that to find out a way of your own was—Besides, there is no new way out."

"So it is always supposed."

"Except through the vomitories, for which one must have an Egression-permit, it is impossible to get out. The Book says so."

"Well, the Book's wrong, for I have been out on my feet."

For Kuno was possessed of a certain physical strength.

By these days it was a demerit to be muscular. Each infant was examined at birth, and all who promised undue strength were destroyed. Humanitarians may protest, but it would have been no true kindness to let an athlete live; he would never have been happy in that state of life to which the Machine had called him; he would have yearned for trees to climb, rivers to bathe in, meadows and hills against which he might measure his body. Man must be adapted to his surroundings, must he not? In the dawn of the world our weakly must be exposed on Mount Taygetus, in its twilight our strong will suffer euthanasia, that the Machine may progress, that the Machine may progress, that the Machine may progress eternally.

"You know that we have lost the sense of space. We say 'space is annihilated,' but we have annihilated not space, but the sense thereof. We have lost a part of ourselves. I determined to recover it, and I began by walking up and down the platform of the railway outside my room. Up and down, until I was tired, and so did recapture the meaning of 'Near' and 'Far.' 'Near' is a place to which I can get quickly *on my feet*, not a place to which the train or the air-ship will take me quickly. 'Far' is a place to which I cannot get quickly on my feet; the vomitory is 'far,' though I could be there in thirty-eight seconds by summoning the train. Man is the measure. That was my first lesson. Man's feet are the measure for distance, his hands are the measure for ownership, his body is the measure for all that is lovable and desirable and strong. Then I went further: it was then that I called to you for the first time, and you would not come.

"This city, as you know, is built deep beneath the surface of the earth, with only the vomitories protruding. Having paced the platform outside my own room, I took the lift to the next platform and paced that also, and so with each in turn, until I came to the topmost, above which begins the earth. All the platforms were exactly alike, and all that I gained by visiting them was to develop my sense of space and my muscles. I think I should have been content with this—it is not a little thing—but as I walked and brooded, it occurred to me that our cities had been built in the days when men still breathed the outer air, and that there had been ventilation shafts for the workmen. I could think of nothing but these ventilation shafts. Had they been destroyed by all the food-tubes and medicine-tubes and music-tubes that the Machine has evolved lately? Or did traces of them remain? One thing was certain. If I came upon them anywhere, it would be in the railway-tunnels of the topmost story. Everywhere else, all space was accounted for.

"I am telling my story quickly, but don't think that I was not a coward or that your answers never depressed me. It is not the proper thing, it is not mechanical, it is not decent to walk along a railway-tunnel. I did not fear that I might tread upon a live rail and be killed. I feared something far more intangible—doing what was not contemplated by the Machine. Then I said to myself, 'Man is the measure,' and I went, and after many visits I found an opening.

"The tunnels, of course, were lighted. Everything is light, artificial light; darkness is the exception. So when I saw a black gap in the tiles, I knew that it was an exception, and rejoiced. I put in my arm—I could put in no more at first—and waved it round and round in ecstasy. I loosened another tile, and put in my head, and shouted into the darkness: 'I am coming, I shall do it yet,' and my voice reverberated down endless passages. I seemed to hear the spirits of those dead workmen who had returned each evening to the starlight and to their wives, and all the generations who had lived in the open air called back to me, 'You will do it yet, you are coming.'"

He paused, and, absurd as he was, his last words moved her. For Kuno had lately asked to be a father, and his request had been refused by the Committee. His was not a type that the Machine desired to hand on.

"Then a train passed. It brushed by me, but I thrust my head and arms into the hole. I had done enough for one day, so I crawled back to the platform, went down in the lift, and summoned my bed. Ah, what dreams! And again I called you, and again you refused."

She shook her head and said:

"Don't. Don't talk of these terrible things. You make me miserable. You are throwing civilisation away."

"But I had got back the sense of space and a man cannot rest then. I determined to get in at the hole and climb the shaft. And so I exercised my arms. Day after day I went through ridiculous movements, until my flesh ached, and I could hang by my hands and hold the pillow of my bed outstretched for many minutes. Then I summoned a respirator, and started.

"It was easy at first. The mortar had somehow rotted, and I soon pushed some more tiles in, and clambered after them into the darkness, and the spirits of the dead comforted me. I don't know what I mean by that. I just say what I felt. I felt, for the first time, that a protest had been lodged against corruption, and that even as the dead were comforting me, so I was comforting the unborn. I felt that humanity existed, and that it existed without clothes. How can I possibly explain this? It was naked, humanity seemed naked, and all these tubes and buttons and machineries neither came into the world with us, nor will they follow us out, nor do they matter supremely while we are here. Had I been strong, I would have torn off every garment I had, and gone out into the outer air unswaddled. But this is not for me, nor perhaps for my generation. I climbed with my respirator and my hygienic clothes and my dietetic tabloids! Better thus than not at all.

"There was a ladder, made of some primæval metal. The light from the railway fell upon its lowest rungs, and I saw that it led straight upwards out of the rubble at the bottom of the shaft. Perhaps our ancestors ran up and down it a dozen times daily, in their building. As I climbed, the rough edges cut through my gloves so that my hands bled. The light helped me for a little, and then came darkness and, worse still, silence which pierced my ears like a sword. The Machine hums! Did you know that? Its hum penetrates our blood, and may even guide our thoughts. Who knows! I was getting beyond its power. Then I thought: 'This silence means that I am doing wrong.' But I heard voices in the silence, and again they strengthened me." He laughed. "I had need of them. The next moment I cracked my head against something."

She sighed.

"I had reached one of those pneumatic stoppers that defend us from the outer air. You may have noticed them on the air-ship. Pitch dark, my feet on the rungs of an invisible ladder, my hands cut; I cannot explain how I lived through this part, but the voices still comforted me, and I felt for fastenings. The stopper, I suppose, was about eight feet across. I passed my hand over it as far as I could reach. It was perfectly smooth. I felt it almost to the centre. Not quite to the centre, for my arm was too short. Then the voice said: 'Jump. It is worth it. There may be a handle in the centre, and you may catch hold of it and so come to us your own way. And if there is no handle, so that you may fall and are dashed to pieces—it is still worth it: you will still come to us your own way.' So I jumped. There was a handle, and—"

He paused. Tears gathered in his mother's eyes. She knew that he was fated. If he did not die today he would die tomorrow. There was not room for such a person in the world. And with her pity disgust mingled. She was ashamed at having borne such a son, she who had always been so respectable and so full of ideas. Was he really the little boy to whom she had taught the use of his stops and buttons, and to whom she had given his first lessons in the Book? The very hair that disfigured his lip showed that he was reverting to some savage type. On atavism the Machine can have no mercy.

"There was a handle, and I did catch it. I hung tranced over the darkness and heard the hum of these workings as the last whisper in a dying dream. All the things I had cared about and all the people I had spoken to through tubes appeared infinitely little. Meanwhile the handle revolved. My weight had set something in motion and I span slowly, and then—

"I cannot describe it. I was lying with my face to the sunshine. Blood poured from my nose and ears and I heard a tremendous roaring. The stopper, with me clinging to it, had simply been blown out of the earth, and the air that we make down here was escaping through the vent into the air above. It burst up like a fountain. I crawled back to it—for the upper air hurts—and, as it were, I took great sips from the edge. My respirator had flown goodness knows where, my clothes were torn. I just lay with my lips close to the hole, and I sipped until the bleeding stopped. You can imagine nothing so curious. This hollow in the grass—I will speak of it in a minute,—the sun shining into it, not brilliantly but through marbled clouds,—the peace, the nonchalance, the sense of space, and, brushing my cheek, the roaring fountain of our artificial air! Soon I spied my respirator, bobbing up and down in the current high above my head, and higher still were many air-ships. But no one ever looks out of air-ships, and in my case they could not have picked me up. There I was, stranded. The sun shone a little way down the shaft, and revealed the topmost rung of the ladder, but it was hopeless trying to reach it. I should either have been tossed up again by the escape, or else have fallen in, and died. I could only lie on the grass, sipping and sipping, and from time to time glancing around me.

"I knew that I was in Wessex, for I had taken care to go to a lecture on the subject before starting. Wessex lies above the room in which we are talking now. It was once an important state. Its kings held all the southern coast from the Andredswald to Cornwall, while the Wansdyke protected them on the north, running over the high ground. The lecturer was only concerned with the rise of Wessex, so I do not know how long it remained an international power, nor would the knowledge have assisted me. To tell the truth I could do nothing but laugh, during this part. There was I, with a pneumatic stopper by my side and a respirator bobbing over my head, imprisoned, all three of us, in a grass-grown hollow that was edged with fern."

Then he grew grave again.

"Lucky for me that it was a hollow. For the air began to fall back into it and to fill it as water fills a bowl. I could crawl about. Presently I stood. I breathed a mixture, in which the air that hurts predominated whenever I tried to climb the sides. This was not so bad. I had not lost my tabloids and remained ridiculously cheerful, and as for the Machine, I forgot about it altogether. My one aim now was to get to

the top, where the ferns were, and to view whatever objects lay beyond.

"I rushed the slope. The new air was still too bitter for me and I came rolling back, after a momentary vision of something grey. The sun grew very feeble, and I remembered that he was in Scorpio—I had been to a lecture on that too. If the sun is in Scorpio and you are in Wessex, it means that you must be as quick as you can, or it will get too dark. (This is the first bit of useful information I have ever got from a lecture, and I expect it will be the last.) It made me try frantically to breathe the new air, and to advance as far as I dared out of my pond. The hollow filled so slowly. At times I thought that the fountain played with less vigour. My respirator seemed to dance nearer the earth; the roar was decreasing."

He broke off.

"I don't think this is interesting you. The rest will interest you even less. There are no ideas in it, and I wish that I had not troubled you to come. We are too different, mother."

She told him to continue.

"It was evening before I climbed the bank. The sun had very nearly slipped out of the sky by this time, and I could not get a good view. You, who have just crossed the Roof of the World, will not want to hear an account of the little hills that I saw—low colourless hills. But to me they were living and the turf that covered them was a skin, under which their muscles rippled, and I felt that those hills had called with incalculable force to men in the past, and that men had loved them. Now they sleep—perhaps for ever. They commune with humanity in dreams. Happy the man, happy the woman, who awakes the hills of Wessex. For though they sleep, they will never die."

His voice rose passionately.

"Cannot you see, cannot all your lecturers see, that it is we who are dying, and that down here the only thing that really lives is the Machine? We created the Machine, to do our will, but we cannot make it do our will now. It has robbed us of the sense of space and of the sense of touch, it has blurred every human relation and narrowed down love to a carnal act, it has paralysed our bodies and our wills, and now it compels us to worship it. The Machine develops—but not on our lines. The Machine proceeds—but not to our goal. We only exist as the blood corpuscles that course through its arteries, and if it could work without us, it would let us die. Oh, I have no remedy—or, at least, only one—to tell men again and again that I have seen the hills of Wessex as Ælfrid saw them when he overthrew the Danes.

"So the sun set. I forgot to mention that a belt of mist lay between my hill and other hills, and that it was the colour of pearl."

He broke off for the second time.

"Go on," said his mother wearily.

He shook his head.

"Go on. Nothing that you say can distress me now. I am hardened."

"I had meant to tell you the rest, but I cannot: I know that I cannot: good-bye."

Vashti stood irresolute. All her nerves were tingling with his blasphemies. But she was also inquisitive.

"This is unfair," she complained. "You have called me across the world to hear your story, and hear it I will. Tell me—as briefly as possible, for this is a disastrous waste of time—tell me how you returned to civilisation."

"Oh—that!" he said, starting. "You would like to hear about civilisation. Certainly. Had I got to where my respirator fell down?"

„No—but I understand everything now. You put on your respirator, and managed to walk along the surface of the earth to a vomitory, and there your conduct was reported to the Central Committee."

"By no means."

He passed his hand over his forehead, as if dispelling some strong impression. Then, resuming his narrative, he warmed to it again.

"My respirator fell about sunset. I had mentioned that the fountain seemed feebler, had I not."

"Yes."

"About sunset, it let the respirator fall. As I said, I had entirely forgotten about the Machine, and I paid no great attention at the time, being occupied with other things. I had my pool of air, into which I could dip when the outer keenness became intolerable, and which would possibly remain for days, provided that no wind sprang up to disperse it. Not until it was too late, did I realize what the stoppage of the escape implied. You see—the gap in the tunnel had been mended; the Mending Apparatus; the Mending Apparatus, was after me.

"One other warning I had, but I neglected it. The sky at night was clearer than it had been in the day, and the moon, which was about half the sky behind the sun, shone into the dell at moments quite brightly. I was in my usual place—on the boundary between the two atmospheres—when I thought I saw something dark move across the bottom of the dell, and vanish into the shaft. In my folly, I ran down. I bent over and listened, and I thought I heard a faint scraping noise in the depths.

"At this—but it was too late—I took alarm. I determined to put on my respirator and to walk right out of the dell. But my respirator had gone. I knew exactly where it had fallen—between the stopper and the aperture—and I could even feel the mark that it had made in the turf. It had gone, and I realized that something evil was at work, and I had better escape to the other air, and, if I must die, die running towards the cloud that had been the colour of a pearl. I never started. Out of the shaft—it is too horrible. A worm, a long white worm, had crawled out of the shaft and was gliding over the moonlit grass.

"I screamed. I did everything that I should not have done, I stamped upon the creature instead of flying from it, and it at once curled round the ankle. Then we fought. The worm let me run all over the dell, but edged up my leg as I ran. 'Help!' I cried. (That part is too awful. It belongs to the part that you will never know.) 'Help!' I cried. (Why cannot we suffer in silence?) 'Help!' I cried. Then my feet were wound together, I fell, I was dragged away from the dear ferns and the living hills, and past the great metal stopper (I can tell you this part), and I thought it might save me again if I caught hold of the handle. It also was enwrapped, it also. Oh, the whole dell was full of the things. They were search-ing it in all directions, they were denud-ing it, and the white snouts of others peeped out of the hole, ready if needed. Everything that could be moved they brought—brushwood, bundles of fern, everything, and down we all went inter-twined into hell. The last things that I saw, ere the stopper closed after us, were certain stars, and I felt that a man of my sort lived in the sky. For I did fight, I fought till the very end, and it was only my head hitting against the ladder that quieted me. I woke up in this room. The worms had vanished. I was surrounded by artificial air, artifi-cial light, artificial peace, and my friends were calling to me down speaking-tubes to know whether I had come across any new ideas lately."

Here his story ended. Discussion of it was impossible, and Vashti turned to go.

"It will end in Homelessness," she said quietly.

"I wish it would," retorted Kuno.

"The Machine has been most merciful."

"I prefer the mercy of God."

"By that superstitious phrase, do you mean that you could live in the outer air?"

"Yes."

"Have you ever seen, round the vomitories, the bones of those who were extruded after the Great Rebellion?"

"Yes."

"They were left where they perished for our edification. A few crawled away, but they perished, too—who can doubt it? And so with the Homeless of our own day. The surface of the earth supports life no longer."

„Indeed."

"Ferns and a little grass may survive, but all higher forms have perished. Has any air-ship detected them?"

"No."

"Has any lecturer dealt with them?"

"No."

"Then why this obstinacy?"

"Because I have seen them," he exploded.

„Seen *what*?"

"Because I have seen her in the twilight—because she came to my help when I called—because she, too, was entangled by the worms, and, luckier than I, was killed by one of them piercing her throat."

He was mad. Vashti departed, nor, in the troubles that followed, did she ever see his face again.

PART III
THE HOMELESS

DURING THE YEARS THAT FOLLOWED Kuno's escapade, two important devel-opments took place in the Machine. On the surface they were revolutionary, but in either case men's minds had been prepared beforehand, and they did but express ten-dencies that were latent already.

The first of these was the abolition of respirators.

Advanced thinkers, like Vashti, had always held it foolish to visit the surface of the earth. Air-ships might be necessary, but what was the good of going out for mere curiosity and crawling along for a mile or two in a terrestrial motor? The habit was vulgar and perhaps faintly improper: it was unproductive of ideas, and had no connection with the habits that really mattered. So respirators were abolished, and with them, of course, the terrestrial motors, and except for a few lecturers, who complained that they were debarred access to their subject-matter, the development was accepted quietly. Those who still wanted to know what the earth was like had after all only to listen to some gramophone, or to look into some cinematophote. And even the lecturers acquiesced when they found that a lecture on the sea was none the less stimulating when compiled out of other lectures that had already been delivered on the same subject. "Beware of first-hand ideas!" exclaimed one of the most advanced of them. "First-hand ideas do not really exist. They are but the physical impressions produced by love and fear, and on this gross foundation who could erect a philosophy? Let your ideas be second-hand, and if possible tenth-hand, for then they will be far removed from that disturbing element—direct observation. Do not learn anything about this subject of mine—the French Revolution. Learn instead what I think that Enicharmon thought Urizen thought Gutch thought Ho-Yung thought Chi-Bo-Sing thought Lafcadio Hearn thought Carlyle thought Mirabeau said about the French Revolution. Through the medium of these eight great minds, the blood that was shed at Paris and the windows that were broken at Versailles will be clarified to an idea which you may employ most profitably in your daily lives. But be sure that the intermediates are many and varied, for in history one authority exists to counteract another. Urizen must counteract the scepticism of Ho-Yung and Enicharmon, I must myself counteract the impetuosity of Gutch. You who listen to me are in a better position to judge about the French Revolution than I am. Your descendants will be even in a better position than you, for they will learn what you think I think, and yet another intermediate will be added to the chain. And in time"—his voice rose—"there will come a generation that has got beyond facts, beyond impressions, a generation absolutely colourless, a generation

'seraphically free

From taint of personality,'

which will see the French Revolution not as it happened, nor as they would like it to have happened, but as it would have happened, had it taken place in the days of the Machine."

Tremendous applause greeted this lecture, which did but voice a feeling already latent in the minds of men—a feeling that terrestrial facts must be ignored, and that the abolition of respirators was a positive gain. It was even suggested that air-ships should be abolished too. This was not done, because air-ships had somehow worked themselves into the Machine's system. But year by year they were used less, and mentioned less by thoughtful men.

The second great development was the re-establishment of religion.

This, too, had been voiced in the celebrated lecture. No one could mistake the reverent tone in which the peroration had concluded, and it awakened a responsive echo in the heart of each. Those who had long worshipped silently, now began to talk. They described the strange feeling of peace that came over them when they handled the Book of the Machine, the pleasure that it was to repeat certain numerals out of it, however little meaning those numerals conveyed to the outward ear, the ecstasy of touching a button, however unimport-ant, or of ringing an electric bell, however superfluously.

"The Machine," they exclaimed, "feeds us and clothes us and houses us; through it we speak to one another, through it we see one another, in it we have our being. The Machine is the friend of ideas and the enemy of superstition: the Machine is omnipotent, eternal; blessed is the Machine." And before long this allo-cution was printed on the first page of the Book, and in subsequent editions the ritual swelled into a complicated system of praise and prayer. The word "religion" was sedu-lously avoided, and in theory the Machine was still the creation and the implement of man. But in practice all, save a few retrogrades, worshipped it as divine. Nor was it worshipped in unity. One believer would be chiefly impressed by the blue optic plates, through which he saw other believers; another by the mending appara-tus, which sinful Kuno had compared to worms; another by the lifts, another by the Book. And each would pray to this or to that, and ask it to intercede for him with the Machine as a whole. Persecution—that also was present. It did not break out, for reasons that will be set forward shortly. But it was latent, and all who did not accept the minimum known as "undenominational Mechanism" lived in danger of Homeless-ness, which means death, as we know.

To attribute these two great devel-opments to the Central Committee, is to take a very narrow view of civilisation. The Central Committee announced the devel-opments, it is true, but they were no more the cause of them than were the kings of the imperialistic period the cause of war. Rather did they yield to some invincible pressure, which came no one knew whither, and which, when gratified, was succeeded by some new pressure equally invincible. To such a state of affairs it is convenient to give the name of progress. No one confessed

the Machine was out of hand. Year by year it was served with increased efficiency and decreased intelligence. The better a man knew his own duties upon it, the less he understood the duties of his neighbour, and in all the world there was not one who understood the monster as a whole. Those master brains had perished. They had left full directions, it is true, and their succes-sors had each of them mastered a portion of those directions. But Humanity, in its desire for comfort, had over-reached itself. It had exploited the riches of nature too far. Quietly and complacently, it was sinking into decadence, and progress had come to mean the progress of the Machine.

As for Vashti, her life went peacefully forward until the final disaster. She made her room dark and slept; she awoke and made the room light. She lectured and attended lectures. She exchanged ideas with her innumerable friends and believed she was growing more spiritual. At times a friend was granted Euthanasia, and left his or her room for the homelessness that is beyond all human conception. Vashti did not much mind. After an unsuccess-ful lecture, she would sometimes ask for Euthanasia herself. But the death-rate was not permitted to exceed the birth-rate, and the Machine had hitherto refused it to her.

The troubles began quietly, long before she was conscious of them.

One day she was astonished at receiv-ing a message from her son. They never communicated, having nothing in com-mon, and she had only heard indirectly that he was still alive, and had been trans-ferred from the northern hemisphere, where he had behaved so mischievously, to the southern—indeed, to a room not far from her own.

"Does he want me to visit him?" she thought. "Never again, never. And I have not the time."

No, it was madness of another kind.

He refused to visualize his face upon the blue plate, and speaking out of the darkness with solemnity said:

"The Machine stops."

"What do you say?"

"The Machine is stopping, I know it, I know the signs."

She burst into a peal of laughter. He heard her and was angry, and they spoke no more.

"Can you imagine anything more absurd?" she cried to a friend. "A man who was my son believes that the Machine is stopping. It would be impious if it was not mad."

"The Machine is stopping?" her friend replied. "What does that mean? The phrase conveys nothing to me."

"Nor to me."

"He does not refer, I suppose, to the trouble there has been lately with the music?"

"Oh no, of course not. Let us talk about music."

"Have you complained to the authorities?"

"Yes, and they say it wants mending, and referred me to the Committee of the Mending Apparatus. I complained of those curious gasping sighs that disfigure the symphonies of the Brisbane school. They sound like some one in pain. The Committee of the Mending Apparatus say that it shall be remedied shortly."

Obscurely worried, she resumed her life. For one thing, the defect in the music irritated her. For another thing, she could not forget Kuno's speech. If he had known that the music was out of repair—he could not know it, for he detested music—if he had known that it was wrong, "the Machine stops" was exactly the venomous sort of remark he would have made. Of course he had made it at a venture, but the coincidence annoyed her, and she spoke with some petulance to the Committee of the Mending Apparatus.

They replied, as before, that the defect would be set right shortly.

"Shortly! At once!" she retorted. "Why should I be worried by imperfect music? Things are always put right at once. If you do not mend it at once, I shall complain to the Central Committee."

"No personal complaints are received by the Central Committee," the Committee of the Mending Apparatus replied.

"Through whom am I to make my complaint, then?"

"Through us."

"I complain then."

"Your complaint shall be forwarded in its turn."

"Have others complained?"

This question was unmechanical, and the Committee of the Mending Apparatus refused to answer it.

"It is too bad!" she exclaimed to another of her friends. "There never was such an unfortunate woman as myself. I can never be sure of my music now. It gets worse and worse each time I summon it."

"I too have my troubles," the friend replied. "Sometimes my ideas are interrupted by a slight jarring noise."

"What is it?"

"I do not know whether it is inside my head, or inside the wall."

"Complain, in either case."

"I have complained, and my complaint will be forwarded in its turn to the Central Committee."

Time passed, and they resented the defects no longer. The defects had not been remedied, but the human tissues in that latter day had become so subservient, that they readily adapted themselves to every caprice of the Machine. The sigh at the crisis of the Brisbane symphony no longer irritated Vashti; she accepted it as part of the melody. The jarring noise, whether in the head or in the wall, was no longer resented by her friend. And so with the mouldy artificial fruit, so with the bath water that began to stink, so with the defective rhymes that the poetry machine had taken to emit. All were bitterly complained of at first, and then acquiesced in and forgotten. Things went from bad to worse unchallenged.

It was otherwise with the failure of the sleeping apparatus. That was a more serious stoppage. There came a day when over the whole world—in Sumatra, in Wessex, in the innumerable cities of Courland and Brazil—the beds, when summoned by their tired owners, failed to appear. It may seem a ludicrous matter, but from it we may date the collapse of humanity. The Committee responsible for the failure was assailed by complainants, whom it referred, as usual, to the Committee of the Mending Apparatus, who in its turn assured them that their complaints would be forwarded to the Central Committee. But the discontent grew, for mankind was not yet sufficiently adaptable to do without sleeping.

"Some one is meddling with the Machine—" they began.

"Some one is trying to make himself king, to reintroduce the personal element."

"Punish that man with Homelessness."

"To the rescue! Avenge the Machine! Avenge the Machine!"

"War! Kill the man!"

But the Committee of the Mending Apparatus now came forward, and allayed the panic with well-chosen words. It confessed that the Mending Apparatus was itself in need of repair.

The effect of this frank confession was admirable.

"Of course," said a famous lecturer—he of the French Revolution, who gilded each new decay with splendour—"of course we shall not press our complaints now. The Mending Apparatus has treated us so well in the past that we all sympathize with it, and will wait patiently for its recovery. In its own good time it will resume its duties.

Meanwhile let us do without our beds, our tabloids, our other little wants. Such, I feel sure, would be the wish of the Machine."

Thousands of miles away his audience applauded. The Machine still linked them. Under the seas, beneath the roots of the mountains, ran the wires through which they saw and heard, the enormous eyes and ears that were their heritage, and the hum of many workings clothed their thoughts in one garment of subserviency. Only the old and the sick remained ungrateful, for it was rumoured that Euthanasia, too, was out of order, and that pain had reappeared among men.

It became difficult to read. A blight entered the atmosphere and dulled its luminosity. At times Vashti could scarcely see across her room. The air, too, was foul. Loud were the complaints, impotent the remedies, heroic the tone of the lecturer as he cried: "Courage, courage! What matter so long as the Machine goes on? To it the darkness and the light are one." And though things improved again after a time, the old brilliancy was never recaptured, and humanity never recovered from its entrance into twilight. There was an hysterical talk of "measures," of "provisional dictatorship," and the inhabitants of Sumatra were asked to familiarize themselves with the workings of the central power station, the said power station being situated in France. But for the most part panic reigned, and men spent their strength praying to their Books, tangible proofs of the Machine's omnipotence. There were gradations of terror—at times came rumours of hope—the Mending Apparatus was almost mended—the enemies of the Machine had been got under—new "nerve-centres" were evolving which would do the work even more magnificently than before. But there came a day when, without the slightest warning, without any previous hint of feebleness, the entire communication-system broke down, all over the world, and the world, as they understood it, ended.

Vashti was lecturing at the time and her earlier remarks had been punctuated with applause. As she proceeded the audience became silent, and at the conclusion there was no sound. Somewhat displeased, she called to a friend who was a specialist in sympathy. No sound: doubtless the friend was sleeping. And so with the next friend whom she tried to summon, and so with the next, until she remembered Kuno's cryptic remark, "The Machine stops."

The phrase still conveyed nothing. If Eternity was stopping it would of course be set going shortly.

For example, there was still a little light and air—the atmosphere had improved a few hours previously. There was still the Book, and while there was the Book there was security.

Then she broke down, for with the cessation of activity came an unexpected terror—silence.

She had never known silence, and the coming of it nearly killed her—it did kill many thousands of people outright. Ever since her birth she had been surrounded by the steady hum. It was to the ear what artificial air was to the lungs, and agonizing pains shot across her head. And scarcely knowing what she did, she stumbled forward and pressed the unfamiliar button, the one that opened the door of her cell.

Now the door of the cell worked on a simple hinge of its own. It was not connected with the central power station, dying far away in France. It opened, rousing immoderate hopes in Vashti, for she thought that the Machine had been mended. It opened, and she saw the dim tunnel that curved far away towards freedom. One look, and then she shrank back. For the tunnel was full of people—she was almost the last in that city to have taken alarm.

People at any time repelled her, and these were nightmares from her worst dreams. People were crawling about, people were screaming, whimpering, gasping for breath, touching each other, vanishing in the dark, and ever and anon being pushed off the platform on to the live rail. Some were fighting round the electric bells, trying to summon trains which could not be summoned. Others were yelling for Euthanasia or for respirators, or blaspheming the Machine. Others stood at the doors of their cells fearing, like herself, either to stop in them or to leave them. And behind all the uproar was silence—the silence which is the voice of the earth and of the generations who have gone.

No—it was worse than solitude. She closed the door again and sat down to wait for the end. The disintegration went on, accompanied by horrible cracks and rumbling. The valves that restrained the Medical Apparatus must have been weakened, for it ruptured and hung hideously from the ceiling. The floor heaved and fell and flung her from her chair. A tube oozed towards her serpent fashion. And at last the final horror approached—light began to ebb, and she knew that civilisation's long day was closing.

She whirled round, praying to be saved from this, at any rate, kissing the Book, pressing button after button. The uproar outside was increasing, and even penetrated the wall. Slowly the brilliancy of her cell was dimmed, the reflections faded from her metal switches. Now she could not see the reading-stand, now not the Book, though she held it in her hand. Light followed the flight of sound, air was following light, and the original void returned to the cavern from which it had been so long excluded. Vashti continued to whirl, like the devotees of an earlier religion, screaming, praying, striking at the buttons with bleeding hands.

It was thus that she opened her prison and escaped—escaped in the spirit: at least so it seems to me, ere my meditation closes. That she escapes in the body—I cannot perceive that. She struck, by chance, the switch that released the door, and the rush of foul air on her skin, the loud throbbing whispers in her ears, told her that she was facing the tunnel again, and that tremendous platform on which she had seen men fighting. They were not fighting now. Only the whispers remained, and the little whimpering groans. They were dying by hundreds out in the dark.

She burst into tears.

Tears answered her.

They wept for humanity, those two, not for themselves. They could not bear that this should be the end. Ere silence was completed their hearts were opened, and they knew what had been important on the earth. Man, the flower of all flesh, the noblest of all creatures visible, man who had once made god in his image, and had mirrored his strength on the constellations, beautiful naked man was dying, strangled in the garments that he had woven. Century after century had he toiled, and here was his reward. Truly the garment had seemed heavenly at first, shot with the colours of culture, sewn with the threads of self-denial. And heavenly it had been so long as it was a garment and no more, so long as man could shed it at will and live by the essence that is his soul, and the essence, equally divine, that is his body. The sin against the body—it was for that they wept in chief; the centuries of wrong against the muscles and the nerves, and those five portals by which we can alone apprehend—glozing it over with talk of evolution, until the body was white pap, the home of ideas as colourless, last sloshy stirrings of a spirit that had grasped the stars.

"Where are you?" she sobbed.

His voice in the darkness said, "Here."

"Is there any hope, Kuno?"

"None for us."

"Where are you?"

She crawled towards him over the bodies of the dead. His blood spurted over her hands.

"Quicker," he gasped, "I am dying—but we touch, we talk, not through the Machine."

He kissed her.

"We have come back to our own. We die, but we have recaptured life, as it was in Wessex, when Ælfrid overthrew the Danes. We know what they know outside, they who dwelt in the cloud that is the colour of a pearl."

"But, Kuno, is it true? Are there still men on the surface of the earth? Is this—this tunnel, this poisoned darkness—really not the end?"

He replied:

"I have seen them, spoken to them, loved them. They are hiding in the mist and the ferns until our civilisation stops. Today they are the Homeless—tomorrow—"

"Oh, tomorrow—some fool will start the Machine again, tomorrow."

"Never," said Kuno, "never. Humanity has learnt its lesson."

As he spoke, the whole city was broken like a honeycomb. An air-ship had sailed in through the vomitory into a ruined wharf. It crashed downwards, exploding as it went, rending gallery after gallery with its wings of steel. For a moment they saw the nations of the dead, and, before they joined them, scraps of the untainted sky.

THE END

QUEEN OF THE SAGEBRUSH FRONTIER
FIREHAIR
BY JOHN STARR
IT WAS LITTLE AX, SON OF CHIEF TEHAMA, WHO FOUND THE WOUNDED PALEFACE GIRL IN THE WRECKAGE OF A LOOTED WAGON-TRAIN... HER MEMORY WAS DEAD, LOST IN PAIN AND TERROR — SO THE GAVE HER A NEW NAME AND A WILD NEW LIFE BEGAN FOR HER...

LOOK, FIREHAIR — MY ARROW IN THE TARGET! BEAT IT OR SWALLOW YOUR BOASTS!
YOU BABBLE LIKE A FAT PAPOOSE, O RAVEN... STAND BACK!

BEHOLD, MAN-OF-MAGIC — SHE IS STRONG AGAIN... AND WHERE IS THE EVIL YOU FORETOLD SHE WOULD BRING UPON US?

THE WINTER WAS MILD, OUR TRAPS CAUGHT MANY PELTS —

TRUE O TEHAMA! YET MY SMOKE SIGNS SHOW DEATH AND DANGER AROUND HER —
HUSH — SHE SHOOTS!

HAI-EE! RAVEN'S ARROW IN THE FLANK, BUT FIRE-HAIR HAS PIERCED THE EYE!

PALEFACE CHEAT-SHE STEP ACROSS THE LINE!
TONGUE OF A SNAKE! NO ONE CAN SAY I CHEAT!

SO! DOES RAVEN'S COURAGE NEED A KNIFE AGAINST BARE HANDS?
BACK, NAMELESS CUR- OR YOUR FACE SMILES WITH THREE MOUTHS!

THE KNIFE- RAVEN STRIKES.. SHE WILL KILL HER!
AI-EEE- STOP HER!
NO, LOOK! FIREHAIR HAS HER ARM- SHE TWISTS HER BACK..

STOP. HELP!
TAKE HER, POOL, AND WASH HER LIES AWAY!

DEATH AND DANGER AROUND HER, MAGIC-MAN? HAH, I SAY DEATH AND DANGER FOR THOSE WHO DARE TO OPPOSE OUR WARRIOR-MAIDEN, FIREHAIR!

AND THE HIGH SNOWS MELTED, AND THE SPRING SUN SHONE, AND FIREHAIR WAS NO MORE A STRANGER WITHIN TEHAMA'S TRIBE... AND BETWEEN THE WHITE GIRL, AND THE CHIEF'S YOUNG SON, THE BONDS OF FRIENDSHIP GREW...

HO, MY SISTER-QUICK! THE HERD WE TRAILED - I HAVE SIGHTED IT AGAIN... TAKE MY REINS!

THE TEEPEES WILL LAUGH, LITTLE AX, TO SEE THE SISTER RIDE WHILE THE BROTHER GOES AFOOT.
BAH! WHO CARES FOR THE GIGGLES OF FOOLS?

I SWORE BLOOD'S OATH TO CARE FOR YOU UNTIL YOUR MEMORY HEALS... HAVE YOU DREAMED OF THE PAST AGAIN, SISTER?
ONLY TWO THINGS - A VOICE THAT CALLED ME PRINCESS, AND A REACHING HAND OF FEAR... IS THIS THE PLACE?

SOFTLY... THEY GRAZE TOWARD US, WE WILL CREEP DOWN AMONG THE ROCKS -
BUT MY BLAZE-FACE HORSE... I DO NOT SEE HIM.

HE FEEDS ALONG THE CANYON'S EDGE, S-SS-SH - NOT A SOUND!

YES, YES, IT IS BLAZE-FACE, AND EVERY STEP BRINGS HIM CLOSER!
READY YOUR ROPE!

ON THE CANYON FLOOR WARY NOSTRILS SCENT THE WIND.

HOH! HE IS OURS!
GREAT SPIRIT, GUIDE MY CAST... IT MUST NOT MISS!

THE KING OF STALLIONS— AND MINE, MINE!
NOT TOO NEAR, FIREHAIR! SNUB HIM TIGHT! HE HAS DEVILS IN HIS EYES—

LITTLE AX! BEHIND YOU, QUICK!

RUN, BROTHER—
MY BLADE WILL
HARRY HIM
OFF!

BUT EVEN THEN,
THE YOUNG BRAVE'S
BOW WAS TWANGING

WITHOUT YOUR BLADE,
FIREHAIR, IT IS LITTLE-
AX WHO LIES THERE
DEAD!
BUT WITHOUT
YOUR ARROW—LOOK
BROTHER, WHAT
DO I SEE?

OUR TRAILING
ROPES SNAGGED
AS HE RAN!
HOH! THE GREAT
SPIRIT HELD HIM
SAFE FOR YOU!

HE IS STUNNED,
EXHAUSTED...THIS
ROPE FOR A HALTER,
THEN HOBBLE
HIM —
BUT THE DEVILS
ARE STILL IN HIS
EYES, SISTER...YOU
WILL NEVER TAME
HIM!

DEVIL-EYE, SO BE
HIS NAME... AND TIME
WILL TELL IF THE DEVILS
IN HIM CAN OUT-DEVIL
THE DEVILS IN
ME!

AND WITH THE SECOND MOON OF SPRING, THE TRIBES PREPARE FOR THE GREAT ASSEMBLY.. THE PAWNEES LOAD THEIR PELTS, THE BLACKFEET ARE RIDING, TRAIL-FIRES GLEAM IN THE PRAIRIE NIGHT, . AND FROM THE HILLS EVIL EYES WATCH THE CAVALCADES— HUMAN BUZZARDS, SCENTING LOOT AND PLUNDER ...
WITH HOSSFLESH BRINGIN' THREE HUNDRED A HEAD, WE GOT US A GOLD MINE, BOYS! HAVE YUH SPOTTED A LIKELY BUNCH, BLACKIE?
ONE COMIN' YONDER RIGHT NOW, FINGERS... SADDLE UP AN' WE'LL TAKE A LOOK-SEE!

DAKOTAS, HUH? AN' PLENTY FUR ON THEIR POLE-DRAGS, TOO!
BUT LOOKIT TH' CAVVY, FINGERS! I NEVER SEEN A PURTIER BUNCH OF PONIES!

HO, DEVIL—STEADY! WHAT NEXT LITTLE BROTHER?
HOLD THEM IN THE RAVINE UNTIL WE BUILD OUR FENCES...

HEAP PLENTY BRAVES IN THAT PARTY, FINGERS. WON'T A RAID BE RISKY?
NOT WITH OLD CRAZY HORSE TO SIGNAL WHEN THE TIME IS RIPE...

INJUNS ARE GAMBLERS, BLACKIE... ALL NIGHT TONIGHT THEY'LL BE POW-WOWIN', MAKIN' BETS... AN TOMORROW EVERY WARRIOR WILL BE AT THE RACES... THAT'S WHEN WE HIT 'EM, BOY—WITH ONLY THE SQUAWS TO STOP US!

NEXT DAY...
THE PAWNEES RIDE FORTH, O TEHAMA, AND THEIR CHIEF, SPOTTED FACE, HAS SIGN FOR YOU!

GREETINGS, TEHAMA... THERE IS A MAIDEN OF YOUR TRIBE, ONE WITH HAIR OF FIRE, THAT MY FOOLISH SON HAS GAZED UPON—
AH—THERE SHE RIDES, EVEN NOW.

I SEE STORM IN YOUR EYES, SISTER—WHY?
BECAUSE I MUST TEND THE FIRES WHILE THE WARRIORS RACE! BAH, I SAY!

WOULD YOU WAGER HER AGAINST TWENTY HORSES?
ALL THE HORSES OF THE PAWNEE NATION COULD NOT BUY HER, CHIEF... ENOUGH—LET US GO!

I CAN RIDE AS WELL AS ANY BRAVE.. MY DEVIL CAN OUTSPEED ANY PAWNEE HORSE.. YET I MUST SIT IN CAMP LIKE THE AGED CRONES—
EVEN FIREHAIR'S TEMPER CANNOT CHANGE OUR LAWS FAREWELL!

—BUT AS THE WARRIORS RIDE—
LO, THEY CROSS THE CREEK. IT IS TIME FOR SMOKE TO TALK!

IN THE HILLS BEYOND—
THERE SHE BLOWS— OUR SIGN! COAST ALL CLEAR!
BOOTS AN' SADDLES, BOYS!

YOU KNOW THE PLAN, SUNDANCE... RIDE DOWN AN' SPOOK 'EM WHEN WE'VE CLEANED THE WAY!
BUENO, FINGERS!

GIVE 'EM A LITTLE START, BLACKIE...ALL WE GOT TO DO IS BUST TH' FENCE—
YEAH, AN' DODGE THE TOMAHAWKS, BUT I'M READY IF YOU ARE.

SOON...
HO-HO! FIREHAIR WOULD RACE WITH THE BRAVES!
SHOW US YOUR SCALPS, FIREHAIR! PERHAPS SHE WILL LEAD OUR NEXT WAR-PARTY!
LISTEN— GUN- SHOTS!

—FROM BEYOND THE HILLS, FROM THE HORSE PENS!
AND ONLY HALF-GROWN BOYS ON GUARD THERE!

WHITE MEN—THIEVES! OUR BOYS DRIVEN OFF!
GO, DEVIL, GO!

BELOW—
FINGERS—BEHIND YUH! KID SNEAKIN' UP!
NO— WHITE MAN STOP!

SHOTS IN THE AIR DIDN'T SKEER YUH BAD ENOUGH, HUH? OKAY, TRY THIS!
HYAR COMES SUNDOWN'S BUNCH ON THE PROD!

YEE-OW! DRIVE 'EM!
THAT'S THE STUFF, SUNDOWN! KEEP 'EM HUMPIN'!

BUT AS SUNDOWN SPURS AHEAD.
A SQUAW— AA-AGH!

A SQUAW HORSE-THIEF, BUT A BETTER MAN THAN YOU... HAH—HIS GUN!

THE FEEL OF IT IN MY HAND-AS IF I HAD SHOT MANY GUNS BEFORE...BUT WHERE-WHERE?
DRIVE 'EM ON BOYS-I'LL FIX 'ER!

REDHEAD HELLCAT—BULLET NICKED ME! CAN'T DRIVE THE HERD WITH HER ON OUR TAIL!

AND WILD STAMPEDE POUNDS THROUGH THE CAMP AS FINGERS VEERS THE FRENZIED PONIES...

DEVIL-THIEF! AND NOW HE FLEES—THE DUST CLOUDS HIDE HIM—AND MY GUN IS EMPTY!

RIDE WEST, BOYS—SCATTER! THEM BUSTED TEEPEES WILL PAY FOR SHOOTIN' DOWN TEX AN' CACTUS!

LATER...
YOU SEEN THAT REDHEAD SQUAW BEFORE? BUT HOW, BOSS—WHERE?
WAGON TRAIN—OWW—WE RAIDED LAST FALL... WE FIGGERED HER FER DEAD!

YUH MEAN WHEN WE FOUND THAT BLACK STEEL BOX WE COULDN'T FORCE OPEN?
THAT'S IT, BLACKIE—SHE'S THE SAME GAL... WHICH MEANS THERE IS A MURDER NOOSE HUGGIN' OUR NECKS UNTIL SHE'S SENT TO HER HAPPY HUNTIN' GROUNDS!

THE BRIDGE OF SAN LUIS REY

BY THORNTON WILDER

PART FIVE:
PERHAPS AN INTENTION

A NEW BRIDGE OF STONE HAS BEEN BUILT in the place of the old, but the event has not been forgotten. It has passed into proverbial expressions. "I may see you Tuesday," says a Limean, "unless the bridge falls." "My cousin lives by the bridge of San Luis Rey," says another, and a smile goes around the company, for that also means: under the sword of Damocles. There are some poems about the accident, classics to be found in every Peruvian anthology, but the real literary monument is Brother Juniper's book.

There are a hundred ways of wondering at circumstance. Brother Juniper would never have arrived at his method had it not been for his friendship with a certain master in the University of San Martín. This student's wife had stolen away one morning on a boat for Spain, following a soldier, and had left him the care of two daughters in their cradle. He was possessed of all the bitterness that Brother Juniper lacked and derived a sort of joy from the conviction that all was wrong in the world. He whispered into the Franciscan's ear such thoughts and anecdotes as belied the notion of a guided world. For a moment a look of distress, almost of defeat, would come into the Brother's eyes; then he would begin patiently explaining why such stories held no difficulty for a believer. "There was a queen of Naples and Sicily," the student would say, "who discovered that she was carrying an angry tumor in her side. In great dismay she commanded her subjects to fall to their prayers and ordered that all the garments in Sicily and Naples be sewn with votive crosses. She was well loved by her people and all their prayers and embroideries were sincere, but ineffectual. Now she lies in the splendor of Monreale, and a few inches above her heart may be read the words: *I shall fear no evil.*"

It was by dint of hearing a great many such sneers at faith that Brother Juniper became convinced that the world's time had come for proof, tabulated proof, of the

> ## "DO ANY HUMAN BEINGS EVER REALIZE LIFE WHILE THEY LIVE IT -- EVERY, EVERY MINUTE?"
>
> # — THORNTON WILDER
> ## OUR TOWN

conviction that was so bright and exciting within him. When the pestilence visited his dear village of Puerto and carried off a large number of peasants, he secretly drew up a diagram of the characteristics of fifteen victims and fifteen survivors, the statistics of their value *sub specie aeternitatis*. Each soul was rated upon a basis of ten as regards its goodness, its diligence in religious observance, and its importance to its family group. Here is a fragment of this ambitious chart:

	Goodness	Piety	Usefulness
Alfonso G.	4	4	10
Nina	2	5	10
Manuel B.	10	10	0
Alfonso V.	-8	-10	10
Vera N.	0	10	10

The thing was more difficult than he had foreseen. Almost every soul in a difficult frontier community turned out to be indispensable economically, and the third column was all but useless. The examiner was driven to the use of minus terms when he confronted the personal character of Alfonso V., who was not, like Vera N., merely bad: he was a propagandist for badness and not merely avoided church but led others to avoid it. Vera N. was indeed bad, but she was a model worshipper and the mainstay of a full hut. From all this saddening data Brother Juniper contrived an index for each peasant. He added up the total for victims and compared it with the total for survivors, to discover that the dead were five times more worth saving. It almost looked as though the pestilence had been directed against the really valuable people in the village of Puerto. And on that afternoon Brother Juniper took a walk along the edge of the Pacific. He tore up his findings and cast them into the waves; he gazed for an hour upon the great clouds of pearl that hang forever upon the horizon of that sea, and extracted from their beauty a resignation

that he did not permit his reason to examine. The discrepancy between faith and the facts is greater than is generally assumed.

But there was another story of the master of San Martín (not so subversive, this one) that probably gave to Brother Juniper the hint for his procedure after the fall of the bridge of San Luis Rey.

This master was one day walking through the Cathedral of Lima and stopped to read the epitaph of a lady. He read with an increasingly prominent lower lip that she had been for twenty years the centre and joy of her home, that she had been the delight of her friends, that all who met her went away in astonishment at her goodness and beauty, and that there she lay awaiting the return of her Lord. Now on the day that he read these words, the master of San Martín had had much to fret him, and raising his eyes from the tablet he spoke aloud in his rage: "The shame of it, the persecution of it! Everyone knows that in the world we do nothing but feed our wills. Why perpetuate this legend of selflessness? Why keep this thing alive, this rumour of disinterestedness?"

And so saying he resolved to expose this conspiracy of the stone-cutters. The lady had been dead only twelve years. He sought out her servants, her children and her friends. And everywhere he went, like a perfume, her dear traits had survived her and wherever she was mentioned there arose a suffering smile and the protest that words could not describe the gracious ways of her. Even the eager youth of her grandchildren, who had never seen her, was made more difficult by the news that it was possible to be as good as that. And the man stood amazed; only at last he muttered: "Nevertheless, what I said was true. This woman was an exception, perhaps an exception."

In compiling his book about these people Brother Juniper seemed to be pursued by the fear that in omitting the slightest detail he might lose some guiding hint. The longer he worked the more he felt that he was stumbling about among great dim intimations. He was forever being cheated by details that looked as though they were significant if only he could find their setting. So he put everything down on the notion perhaps that if he (or a keener head) reread the book twenty times, the countless facts would suddenly start to move, to assemble, and to betray their secret. The Marquesa de Montemayor's cook told him that she lived almost entirely on rice, fish and a little fruit and Brother Juniper put it down on the chance that it would some day reveal a spiritual trait. Don Rubío said of her that she used to appear at his receptions without invitation in order to steal the spoons. A midwife on the edge of the town declared that Doña María called upon her with morbid questions until she had been obliged to order her away from the door like a beggar. The bookseller of the town reported that she was one of the three most cultivated persons in Lima. Her farmer's wife declared that she was absent-minded, but compact of goodness. The art of biography is more difficult than is generally supposed.

Brother Juniper found that there was least to be learned from those who had been most closely associated with the subjects of his inquiry. Madre María del Pilar talked to him at length about Pepita, but she did not tell him of her own ambitions for her. The Perichole was at first difficult of approach, but presently even liked the Franciscan. Her characterization of Uncle Pio flatly contradicted the stores of unsavory testimonies that he had acquired elsewhere. Her allusions to her son were few and conceded with pain. They closed the interview abruptly. The Captain Alvarado told what he could of Esteban and of Uncle Pio. Those who know most in this realm, venture least.

I shall spare you Brother Juniper's generalizations. They are always with us. He thought he saw in the same accident, the wicked visited by destruction and the good called early to Heaven. He thought he saw

pride and wealth confounded as an object lesson to the world, and he thought he saw humility crowned and rewarded for the edification of the city. But Brother Juniper was not satisfied with his reasons. It was just possible that the Marquesa de Montemayor was not a monster of avarice, and Uncle Pio of self-indulgence.

The book being done fell under the eyes of some judges and was suddenly pronounced heretical. It was ordered to be burned in the Square with its author. Brother Juniper submitted to the decision that the devil had made use of him to effect a brilliant campaign in Peru. He sat in his cell that last night trying to seek in his own life the pattern that had escaped him in five others. He was not rebellious. He was willing to lay down his life for the purity of the church, but he longed for one voice somewhere to testify for him that his intention, at least, had been for faith; he thought there was no one in the world who believed him. But the next morning in all that crowd and sunlight there were many who believed, for he was much loved.

There was a little delegation from the village of Puerto, and Nina (Goodness 2, Piety 5, Usefulness 10) and others stood with drawn puzzled faces while their little friar was given to the congenial flames. Even then, even then, there remained in his heart an obstinate nerve insisting that at least St. Francis would not utterly have condemned him, and (not daring to call upon a greater name, since he seemed so open to error in these matters) he called twice upon St. Francis I and leaning upon a flame he smiled and died.

THE DAY OF THE SERVICE WAS CLEAR AND warm. The Limeans, their black eyes wide with awe, poured through the streets into their Cathedral and stood gazing at the mound of black velvet and silver. The

Archbishop enclosed in his wonderful and almost wooden vestments perspired upon his throne, lending from time to time a connoisseur's ear to the felicities of Vittoria's counterpoint. The choir had restudied the pages that, as his farewell to music, Tomás Luis had composed for his friend and patron, the Empress of Austria, and all that grief and sweetness, all that Spanish realism filtering through an Italian mode, rose and fell above the sea of mantillas. Don. Andrés, under the colours and feathered hangings of his office, knelt, ill and troubled. He knew that the crowd was furtively glancing at him, expecting him to play the father who has lost his only son. He wondered whether the Perichole was present. He had never been obliged to go so long without smoking. The Captain Alvarado pushed in from the sunny square for a moment. He looked across the fields of black hair and lace at the trooping of the candles and the ropes of incense. "How false, how unreal," he said and pushed his way out. He descended to the sea and sat on the edge of his boat, gazing down into the clear water. "Happy are the drowned, Esteban," he said.

Behind the screen the Abbess sat among her girls. The night before she had torn an idol from her heart and the experience had left her pale but firm. She had accepted the fact that it was of no importance whether her work went on or not; it was enough to work. She was the nurse who tends the sick who never recover; she was the priest who perpetually renews the office before an altar to which no worshippers come. There would be no Pepita to enlarge her work; it would relapse into the indolence and the indifference of her colleagues. It seemed to be sufficient for Heaven that for a while in Peru a disinterested love had flowered and faded. She leaned her forehead upon her hand, following the long tender curve that the soprano lifts in the Kyrie. "My affection should have had more of that colour, Pepita. My whole life should have had more of that

quality. I have been too busy," she added ruefully and her mind drifted into prayer.

Camila had started from the farm to attend the service. Her heart was filled with consternation and amazement. Here was another comment from the skies; that was the third time she had been spoken to. Her small-pox, Jaime's illness, and now the fall of the bridge,—oh, these were not accidents. She was as ashamed as though letters had appeared on her forehead. An order from the Palace announced that the Viceroy was sending her two daughters to a convent-school in Spain. That was right. She was alone. She gathered a few things together mechanically and started to the city for the Service. But she fell to thinking of the crowds gaping over her Uncle Pio and over her son; she thought of the vast ritual of the church, like a chasm into which the beloved falls, and of the storm of the *dies irae* where the individual is lost among the millions of the dead, features grow dim and traits fade. At a little more than half the journey, at the mud church of San Luis Rey she slipped in and knelt against a pillar to rest. She wandered through her memory, searching for the faces of her two. She waited for some emotion to appear. "But I feel nothing," she whispered to herself. "I have no heart. I am a poor meaningless woman, that's all. I am shut out. I have no heart. Look, I won't try and think of anything; let me just rest here." And scarcely had she paused when again that terrible incommunicable pain swept through her, the pain that could not speak once to Uncle Pio and tell him of her love and just once offer her courage to Jaime in his sufferings. She started up wildly: "I fail everybody," she cried. "They love me and I fail them." She returned to the farm and carried for a year the mood of her self-despair. One day she heard by accident that the wonderful Abbess had lost two persons whom she loved in the same accident. Her sewing fell from her hand: then she would know, she would explain. "But no, what would she say to me! She would not even believe that such a person as I could love or could lose." Camila decided to go to Lima and look at the Abbess from a distance. "If her face tells me that she would not despise me, I will speak to her," she said.

Camila lurked about the convent church and fell humbly in love with the homely old face, though it frightened her a little. At last she called upon her.

"Mother," she said, "I ... I ..."

"Do I know you, my daughter?"

"I was the actress, I was the Perichole."

"Oh, yes. Oh, I have wished to know you for a long while, but they told me you did not wish to be seen. You too, I know, lost in the fall of the bridge of San...."

Camila rose and swayed. There! again that access of pain, the hands of the dead she could not reach. Her lips were white. Her head brushed the Abbess's knee: "Mother, what shall I do? I am all alone. I have nothing in the world. I love them. What shall I do?"

The Abbess looked at her closely. "My daughter, it is warm here. Let us go into the garden. You can rest there." She made a sign to a girl in the cloister to bring some water. She continued talking mechanically to Camila. "I have wished to know you for a long while, señora. Even before the accident I had wished much to know you. They told me that in the *autos sacrementales* you were a very great and beautiful actress, in *Belshazzar's Feast.*"

"Oh, Mother, you must not say that. I am a sinner. You must not say that."

"Here, drink this, my child. We have a beautiful garden, do you not think so? You will come and see us often and some day you will meet Sister Juana who is our gardener-in-chief. Before she entered religion she had almost never seen a garden, for she worked in the mines high up in the mountains. Now everything grows under her hand.—A year has gone by, señora, since our accident. I lost two who had been

children in my orphanage, but you lost a real child of your own?"

"Yes, Mother."

"And a great friend?"

"Yes, Mother."

"Tell me...."

And then the whole tide of Camila's long despair, her lonely obstinate despair since her girlhood, found its rest on that dusty friendly lap among Sister Juana's fountains and roses.

BUT WHERE ARE SUFFICIENT BOOKS TO CONtain the events that would not have been the same without the fall of the bridge? From such a number I choose one more.

"The Condesa d'Abuirre wishes to see you," said a lay-sister at the door of the Abbess's office.

"Well," said the Abbess, laying down her pen, "who is she?"

"She has just come from Spain. I don't know."

"Oh, it is some money, Inez, some money for my house for the blind. Quick, bid her come in."

The tall, rather languorous beauty entered the room. Doña Clara, who was generally so adequate, seemed constrained for once. "Are you busy, dear Mother, may I talk to you for a while?"

"I am quite free, my daughter. You will excuse an old woman's memory; have I known you before?"

"My mother was the Marquesa de Montemayor...." Doña Clara suspected that the Abbess had not admired her mother and would not let the older woman speak until she herself had made a long passionate defense of Doña María. The languor fell away in her self-reproach. At last the Abbess told her of Pepita and Esteban, and of Camila's visit. "All, all of us have failed. One wishes to be punished. One is willing to assume all kinds of penance, but do you know, my daughter, that in love—I scarcely dare say it—but in love our very mistakes don't seem to be able to last long?"

The Condesa showed the Abbess Doña María's last letter. Madre María dared not say aloud how great her astonishment was that such words (words that since then the whole world has murmured over with joy) could spring in the heart of Pepita's mistress. "Now learn," she commanded herself, "learn at last that anywhere you may expect grace." And she was filled with happiness like a girl at this new proof that the traits she lived for were everywhere, that the world was ready. "Will you do me a kindness, my daughter? Will you let me show you my work?"

The sun had gone down, but the Abbess led the way with a lantern down corridor after corridor. Doña Clara saw the old and the young, the sick and the blind, but most of all she saw the tired, bright old woman who was leading her. The Abbess would stop in a passageway and say suddenly: "I can't help thinking that something could be done for the deaf-and-dumb. It seems to me that some patient person could, ... could study out a language for them. You know there are hundreds and hundreds in Peru. Do you remember whether anyone in Spain has found a way for them? Well, some day they will." Or a little later: "Do you know, I keep thinking that something can be done for the insane. I am old, you know, and I cannot go where these things are talked about, but I watch them sometimes and it seems to me ... In Spain, now, they are gentle with them? It seems to me that there is a secret about it, just hidden from us, just around the corner. Some day back in Spain, if you hear of anything that would help us, you will write me a letter ... if you are not too busy?"

At last after Doña Clara had seen even the kitchens, the Abbess said: "Now will you excuse me, for I must go into the room of the very sick and say a few words for them to think about when they cannot sleep. I will not ask you to come with me there, for you are not accustomed to such ... such sounds and things. And besides I only talk to them as one talks to children." She looked up at her with her modest rueful smile. Suddenly she disappeared a moment to return with one of her helpers, one who had likewise been involved in the affair of the bridge and who had formerly been an actress. "She is leaving me," said the Abbess, "for some work across the city and when I have spoken here I must leave you both, for the flour-broker will not wait for me any longer, and our argument will take a long time."

But Doña Clara stood in the door as the Abbess talked to them, the lamp placed on the floor beside her. Madre María stood with her back against a post; the sick lay in rows gazing at the ceiling and trying to hold their breaths. She talked that night of all those out in the dark (she was thinking of Esteban alone, she was thinking of Pepita alone) who had no one to turn to, for whom the world perhaps was more than difficult, without meaning. And those who lay in their beds there felt that they were within a wall that the Abbess had built for them; within all was light and warmth, and without was the darkness they would not exchange even for a relief from pain and from dying. But even while she was talking, other thoughts were passing in the back of her mind. "Even now," she thought, "almost no one remembers Esteban and Pepita, but myself. Camila alone remembers her Uncle Pio and her son; this woman, her mother. But soon we shall die and all memory of those five will have left the earth, and we ourselves shall be loved for a while and forgotten. But the love will have been enough; all those impulses of love return to the love that made them. Even memory is not necessary for love. There is a land of the living and a land of the dead and the bridge is love, the only survival, the only meaning."

THE END

THE ADVENTURES OF PENROD

BY BOOTH TARKINGTON

CHAPTER XII
MISS RENNSDALE ACCEPTS

"One-two-three; one-two-three—glide!" said Professor Bartet, emphasizing his instructions by a brisk collision of his palms at "glide." "One-two-three; one-two-three—glide!"

The school week was over, at last, but Penrod's troubles were not.

Round and round the ballroom went the seventeen struggling little couples of the Friday Afternoon Dancing Class. Round and round went their reflections with them, swimming rhythmically in the polished, dark floor—white and blue and pink for the girls; black, with dabs of white, for the white-collared, white-gloved boys; and sparks and slivers of high light everywhere as the glistening pumps flickered along the surface like a school of flying fish. Every small pink face—with one exception—was painstaking and set for duty. It was a conscientious little merry-go-round.

"One-two-three; one-two-three—glide! One-two-three; one-two-three—glide! One-two-th—Ha! Mister Penrod Schofield, you lose the step. Your left foot! No, no! This is the left! See—like me! Now again! One-two-three; one-two-three—glide! Better! Much better! Again! One-two-three; one-two-three—gl—Stop! Mr. Penrod Schofield,

this dancing class is provided by the kind parents of the pupilses as much to learn the mannerss of good societies as to dance. You think you shall ever see a gentleman in good societies to tickle his partner in the dance till she say Ouch? Never! I assure you it is not done. Again! Now then! Piano, please! One-two-three; one-two-three—glide! Mr. Penrod Schofield, your right foot—your right foot! No, no! Stop!"

The merry-go-round came to a standstill.

"Mr. Penrod Schofield and partner"—Professor Bartet wiped his brow—"will you kindly observe me? One-two-three—glide! So! Now then—no; you will please keep your places, ladies and gentlemen. Mr. Penrod Schofield, I would puttickly like your attention, this is for you!"

"Pickin' on me again!" murmured the smouldering Penrod to his small, unsympathetic partner. "Can't let me alone a minute!"

"Mister Georgie Bassett, please step to the centre," said the professor.

Mr. Bassett complied with modest alacrity.

"Teacher's pet!" whispered Penrod hoarsely. He had nothing but contempt for Georgie Bassett. The parents, guardians, aunts, uncles, cousins, governesses, housemaids, cooks, chauffeurs and coachmen, appertaining to the members of the dancing class, all dwelt in the same part of town and shared certain communal theories; and among the most firmly established was that which maintained Georgie Bassett to be the Best Boy in Town. Contrariwise, the unfortunate Penrod, largely because of his recent dazzling but disastrous attempts to control forces far beyond him, had been given a clear title as the Worst Boy in Town. (Population, 135,000.) To precisely what degree his reputation was the product of his own energies cannot be calculated. It was Marjorie Jones who first applied the description, in its definite simplicity, the day after the "pageant," and, possibly, her frequent and effusive repetitions of it, even upon wholly irrelevant occasions, had something to do with its prompt and quite perfect acceptance by the community.

"Miss Rennsdale will please do me the fafer to be Mr. Georgie Bassett's partner for one moment," said Professor Bartet. "Mr. Penrod Schofield will please give his attention. Miss Rennsdale and Mister Bassett, obliche me, if you please. Others please watch. Piano, please! Now then!"

Miss Rennsdale, aged eight—the youngest lady in the class—and Mr. Georgie Bassett one-two-three—glided with consummate technique for the better education of Penrod Schofield. It is possible that amber-curled, beautiful Marjorie felt that she, rather than Miss Rennsdale, might have been selected as the example of perfection—or perhaps her remark was only woman.

"Stopping everybody for that boy!" said Marjorie.

Penrod, across the circle from her, heard distinctly—nay, he was obviously intended to hear; but over a scorched heart he preserved a stoic front. Whereupon Marjorie whispered derisively in the ear of her partner, Maurice Levy, who wore a pearl pin in his tie.

"Again, please, everybody—ladies and gentlemen!" cried Professor Bartet.

"Mister Penrod Schofield, if you please, pay puttickly attention! Piano, please! Now then!"

The lesson proceeded. At the close of the hour Professor Bartet stepped to the centre of the room and clapped his hands for attention.

"Ladies and gentlemen, if you please to seat yourselves quietly," he said; "I speak to you now about to-morrow. As you all know—Mister Penrod Schofield, I am not sticking up in a tree outside that window! If you do me the fafer to examine I am here, insides of the room. Now then! Piano, pl—no, I do not wish the piano! As you all know, this is the last lesson of the season until next October. Tomorrow is our special afternoon; beginning three o'clock, we dance the cotillon. But this afternoon comes the test of mannerss. You must see if each know how to make a little formal call like a grown-up people in good societies. You have had good, perfect instruction; let us see if we know how to perform like societies ladies and gentlemen twenty-six years of age.

"Now, when you're dismissed each lady will go to her home and prepare to receive a call. The gentlemen will allow the ladies time to reach their houses and to prepare to receive callers; then each gentleman will call upon a lady and beg the pleasure to engage her for a partner in the cotillon to-morrow. You all know the correct, proper form for these calls, because didn't I work teaching you last lesson till I thought I would drop dead? Yes! Now each gentleman, if he reach a lady's house behind some-other gentleman, then he must go somewhere else to a lady's house, and keep calling until he secures a partner; so, as there are the same number of both, everybody shall have a partner.

"Now please all remember that if in case—Mister Penrod Schofield, when you make your call on a lady I beg you

to please remember that gentlemen in good societies do not scratch the back in societies as you appear to attempt; so please allow the hands to rest carelessly in the lap. Now please all remember that if in case—Mister Penrod Schofield, if you please! Gentlemen in societies do not scratch the back by causing frictions between it and the back of your chair, either! Nobody else is itching here! *I* do not itch! I cannot talk if you must itch! In the name of Heaven, why must you always itch? What was I saying? Where ah! the cotillon—yes! For the cotillon it is important nobody shall fail to be here tomorrow; but if any one should be so very ill he cannot possible come he must write a very polite note of regrets in the form of good societies to his engaged partner to excuse himself—and he must give the reason.

"I do not think anybody is going to be that sick to-morrow—no; and I will find out and report to parents if anybody would try it and not be. But it is important for the cotillon that we have an even number of so many couples, and if it

should happen that someone comes and her partner has sent her a polite note that he has genuine reasons why he cannot come, the note must be handed at once to me, so that I arrange some other partner. Is all understood? Yes. The gentlemen will remember now to allow the ladies plenty of time to reach their houses and prepare to receive calls. Ladies and gentlemen, I thank you for your polite attention."

It was nine blocks to the house of Marjorie Jones; but Penrod did it in less than seven minutes from a flying start—such was his haste to lay himself and his hand for the cotillon at the feet of one who had so recently spoken unamiably of him in public. He had not yet learned that the only safe male rebuke to a scornful female is to stay away from her—especially if that is what she desires. However, he did not wish to rebuke her; simply and ardently he wished to dance the cotillon with her. Resentment was swallowed up in hope.

The fact that Miss Jones' feeling for him bore a striking resemblance to that of Simon Legree for Uncle Tom, deterred him not at all. Naturally, he was not wholly unconscious that when he should lay his hand for the cotillon at her feet it would be her inward desire to step on it; but he believed that if he were first in the field Marjorie would have to accept. These things are governed by law.

It was his fond intention to reach her house even in advance of herself, and with grave misgiving he beheld a large automobile at rest before the sainted gate. Forthwith, a sinking feeling became a portent inside him as little Maurice Levy emerged from the front door of the house.

",Lo, Penrod!" said Maurice airily.

"What you doin' in there?" inquired Penrod.

"In where?"

"In Marjorie's."

"Well, what shouldn't I be doin' in Marjorie's?" Mr. Levy returned indignantly. "I was inviting her for my partner in the cotillon—what you s'pose?"

"You haven't got any right to!" Penrod protested hotly. "You can't do it yet."

"I did do it yet!" said Maurice.

"You can't!" insisted Penrod. "You got to allow them time first. He said the ladies had to be allowed time to prepare."

"Well, ain't she had time to prepare?"

"When?" Penrod demanded, stepping close to his rival threateningly. "I'd like to know when—"

"When?" echoed the other with shrill triumph. "When? Why, in mamma's sixty-horse powder limousine automobile, what Marjorie came home with me in! I guess that's when!"

An impulse in the direction of violence became visible upon the countenance of Penrod.

"I expect you need some wiping down," he began dangerously. "I'll give you sumpthing to remem—"

"Oh, you will!" Maurice cried with astonishing truculence, contorting himself into what he may have considered a posture of defense. "Let's see you try it, you—you itcher!"

For the moment, defiance from such a source was dumfounding. Then, luckily, Penrod recollected something and glanced at the automobile.

Perceiving therein not only the alert chauffeur but the magnificent outlines of Mrs. Levy, his enemy's mother, he manoeuvred his lifted hand so that it seemed he had but meant to scratch his ear.

"Well, I guess I better be goin'," he said casually. "See you tomorrow!"

Maurice mounted to the lap of luxury, and Penrod strolled away with an assumption of careless ease which was put to a severe strain when, from the rear window of the car, a sudden protuberance in the nature of a small, dark, curly head shrieked scornfully:

"Go on—you big stiff!"

The cotillon loomed dismally before Penrod now; but it was his duty to secure a partner and he set about it with a dreary heart. The delay occasioned by his fruitless attempt on Marjorie and the altercation with his enemy at her gate had allowed other ladies ample time to prepare for callers—and to receive them. Sadly he went from house to house, finding that he had been preceded in one after the other. Altogether his hand for the cotillon was declined eleven times that afternoon on the legitimate ground of previous engagement. This, with Marjorie, scored off all except five of the seventeen possible partners; and four of the five were also sealed away from him, as he learned in chance encounters with other boys upon the street.

One lady alone remained; he bowed to the inevitable and entered this lorn damsel's gate at twilight with an air of great discouragement. The lorn damsel was Miss Rennsdale, aged eight.

We are apt to forget that there are actually times of life when too much youth is a handicap. Miss Rennsdale was beautiful; she danced like a premiere; she had every charm but age. On that account alone had she been allowed so much time to prepare to receive callers that it was only by the most manful efforts she could keep her lip from trembling.

A decorous maid conducted the long-belated applicant to her where she sat upon a sofa beside a nursery governess. The decorous maid announced him composedly as he made his entrance.

"Mr. Penrod Schofield!"

Miss Rennsdale suddenly burst into loud sobs.

"Oh!" she wailed. "I just knew it would be him!"

The decorous maid's composure vanished at once—likewise her decorum. She clapped her hand over her mouth and fled, uttering sounds. The governess, however, set herself to comfort her heartbroken charge, and presently succeeded in restoring Miss Rennsdale to a semblance of that poise with which a lady receives callers and accepts invitations to dance cotillons. But she continued to sob at intervals.

Feeling himself at perhaps a disadvantage, Penrod made offer of his hand for the morrow with a little embarrassment. Following the form prescribed by Professor Bartet, he advanced several paces toward the stricken lady and bowed formally.

"I hope," he said by rote, "you're well, and your parents also in good health. May I have the pleasure of dancing the cotillon as your partner t'-morrow afternoon?"

The wet eyes of Miss Rennsdale searched his countenance without pleasure, and a shudder wrung her small shoulders; but the governess whispered to her instructively, and she made a great effort.

"I thu-thank you fu-for your polite invu-invu-invutation; and I ac—" Thus far she progressed when emotion overcame her again. She beat frantically upon the sofa with fists and heels. "Oh, I DID want it to be Georgie Bassett!"

"No, no, no!" said the governess, and whispered urgently, whereupon Miss Rennsdale was able to complete her acceptance.

"And I ac-accept wu-with pu-pleasure!" she moaned, and immediately, uttering a loud yell, flung herself face downward upon the sofa, clutching her governess convulsively.

Somewhat disconcerted, Penrod bowed again.

"I thank you for your polite acceptance," he murmured hurriedly; "and I trust—I trust—I forget. Oh, yes—I trust we shall have a most enjoyable occasion. Pray present my compliments to your parents; and I must now wish you a very good afternoon."

Concluding these courtly demonstrations with another bow he withdrew in fair order, though thrown into partial confusion in the hall by a final wail from his crushed hostess:

"Oh! Why couldn't it be anybody but HIM!"

CHAPTER XIII
THE SMALLPOX MEDICINE

NEXT MORNING PENROD WOKE IN PRO-found depression of spirit, the cotillon ominous before him. He pictured Marjorie Jones and Maurice, graceful and light-hearted, flitting by him fairylike, loosing silvery laughter upon him as he engaged in the struggle to keep step with a partner about four years and two feet his junior. It was hard enough for Penrod to keep step with a girl of his size.

The foreboding vision remained with him, increasing in vividness, throughout the forenoon. He found himself unable to fix his mind upon anything else, and, having bent his gloomy footsteps toward the sawdust-box, after breakfast, presently descended therefrom, abandoning Harold Ramorez where he had left him the preceding Saturday. Then, as he sat communing silently with wistful Duke, in the storeroom, coquettish fortune looked his way.

It was the habit of Penrod's mother not to throw away anything whatsoever until years of storage conclusively proved there would never be a use for it; but a recent house-cleaning had ejected upon the back porch a great quantity of bottles and other paraphernalia of medicine, left over from illnesses in the family during a period of several years. This debris Della, the cook, had collected in a large market basket, adding to it some bottles of flavouring extracts that had proved unpopular in the household; also, old catsup bottles; a jar or two of preserves gone bad; various rejected dental liquids—and other things. And she carried the basket out to the storeroom in the stable.

Penrod was at first unaware of what lay before him. Chin on palms, he sat upon the iron rim of a former aquarium and stared morbidly through the open door at the checkered departing back of Della. It was another who saw treasure in the basket she had left.

Mr. Samuel Williams, aged eleven, and congenial to Penrod in years, sex, and disposition, appeared in the doorway, shaking into foam a black liquid within a pint bottle, stoppered by a thumb.

"Yay, Penrod!" the visitor gave greeting.

"Yay," said Penrod with slight enthusiasm. "What you got?"

"Lickrish water."

"Drinkin's!" demanded Penrod promptly. This is equivalent to the cry of "Biters" when an apple is shown, and establishes unquestionable title.

"Down to there!" stipulated Sam, removing his thumb to affix it firmly as a mark upon the side of the bottle a check upon gormandizing that remained carefully in place while Penrod drank.

This rite concluded, the visitor's eye fell upon the basket deposited by Della. He emitted tokens of pleasure.

"Looky! Looky! Looky there! That ain't any good pile o' stuff—oh, no!"

"What for?"

"Drug store!" shouted Sam. "We'll be partners—"

"Or else," Penrod suggested, "I'll run the drug store and you be a customer—"

"No! Partners!" insisted Sam with such conviction that his host yielded; and within ten minutes the drug store was doing a heavy business with imaginary patrons. Improvising counters with boards and boxes, and setting forth a very druggish-looking stock from the basket, each of the partners found occupation to his taste—Penrod as salesman and Sam as prescription clerk.

"Here you are, madam!" said Penrod briskly, offering a vial of Sam's mixing to an invisible matron. "This will cure your husband in a few minutes. Here's the camphor, mister. Call again! Fifty cents' worth of pills? Yes, madam. There you are! Hurry up with that dose for the nigger lady, Bill!"

"I'll 'tend to it soon's I get time, Jim," replied the prescription clerk. "I'm busy fixin' the smallpox medicine for the sick policeman downtown."

Penrod stopped sales to watch this operation. Sam had found an empty pint bottle and, with the pursed lips and measuring eye of a great chemist, was engaged in filling it from other bottles.

First, he poured into it some of the syrup from the condemned preserves; and a quantity of extinct hair oil; next the remaining contents of a dozen small vials cryptically labelled with physicians' prescriptions; then some remnants of catsup and essence of beef and what was left in several bottles of mouthwash; after that a quantity of rejected flavouring extract—topping off by shaking into the mouth of the bottle various powders from small pink papers, relics of Mr. Schofield's influenza of the preceding winter.

Sam examined the combination with concern, appearing unsatisfied. "We got to make that smallpox medicine good and strong!" he remarked; and, his artistic sense growing more powerful than his appetite, he poured about a quarter of the licorice water into the smallpox medicine.

"What you doin'?" protested Penrod. "What you want to waste that lickrish water for? We ought to keep it to drink when we're tired."

"I guess I got a right to use my own lickrish water any way I want to," replied the prescription clerk. "I tell you, you can't get smallpox medicine too strong. Look at her now!" He held the bottle up admiringly. "She's as black as lickrish. I bet you she's strong all right!"

"I wonder how she tastes?" said Penrod thoughtfully.

"Don't smell so awful much," observed Sam, sniffing the bottle—"a good deal, though!"

"I wonder if it'd make us sick to drink it?" said Penrod.

Sam looked at the bottle thoughtfully; then his eye, wandering, fell upon Duke, placidly curled up near the door, and lighted with the advent of an idea new to him, but old, old in the world—older than Egypt!

"Let's give Duke some!" he cried.

That was the spark. They acted immediately; and a minute later Duke, released from custody with a competent potion of the smallpox medicine inside him, settled conclusively their doubts concerning its effect. The patient animal, accustomed to expect the worst at all times, walked out of the door, shaking his head with an air of considerable annoyance, opening and closing his mouth with singular energy—and so repeatedly that they began to count the number of times he did it. Sam thought it was thirty-nine times, but Penrod had counted forty-one before other and more striking symptoms appeared.

All things come from Mother Earth and must return—Duke restored much at this time. Afterward, he ate heartily of grass; and then, over his shoulder, he bent upon his master one inscrutable look and departed feebly to the front yard.

The two boys had watched the process with warm interest. "I told you she was strong!" said Mr. Williams proudly.

"Yes, sir—she is!" Penrod was generous enough to admit. "I expect she's strong enough—" He paused in thought, and added:

"We haven't got a horse any more."

"I bet you she'd fix him if you had!" said Sam. And it may be that this was no idle boast.

The pharmaceutical game was not resumed; the experiment upon Duke had made the drug store commonplace and stimulated the appetite for stronger meat. Lounging in the doorway, the near-vivisectionists sipped licorice water alternately and conversed.

"I bet some of our smallpox medicine would fix ole P'fessor Bartet all right!" quoth Penrod. "I wish he'd come along and ask us for some."

"We could tell him it was lickrish water," added Sam, liking the idea. "The two bottles look almost the same."

"Then we wouldn't have to go to his ole cotillon this afternoon," Penrod sighed. "There wouldn't be any!"

"Who's your partner, Pen?"

"Who's yours?"

"Who's yours? I just ast you."

"Oh, she's all right!" And Penrod smiled boastfully.

"I bet you wanted to dance with Marjorie!" said his friend.

"Me? I wouldn't dance with that girl if she begged me to! I wouldn't dance with her to save her from drowning! I wouldn't da—"

"Oh, no—you wouldn't!" interrupted Mr. Williams skeptically.

Penrod changed his tone and became persuasive.

"Looky here, Sam," he said confidentially. "I've got 'a mighty nice partner, but my mother don't like her mother; and so I've been thinking I better not dance with her. I'll tell you what I'll do; I've got a mighty good sling in the house, and I'll give it to you if you'll change partners."

"You want to change and you don't even know who mine is!" said Sam, and he made the simple though precocious deduction: "Yours must be a lala! Well, I invited Mabel Rorebeck, and she wouldn't let me change if I wanted to. Mabel Rorebeck'd rather dance with me," he continued serenely, "than anybody; and she said she was awful afraid you'd ast her. But I ain't goin' to dance with Mabel after all,

because this morning she sent me a note about her uncle died last night—and P'fessor Bartet'll have to find me a partner after I get there. Anyway I bet you haven't got any sling—and I bet your partner's Baby Rennsdale!"

"What if she is?" said Penrod. "She's good enough for ME!" This speech held not so much modesty in solution as intended praise of the lady. Taken literally, however, it was an understatement of the facts and wholly insincere.

"Yay!" jeered Mr. Williams, upon whom his friend's hypocrisy was quite wasted. "How can your mother not like her mother? Baby Rennsdale hasn't got any mother! You and her'll be a sight!"

That was Penrod's own conviction; and with this corroboration of it he grew so spiritless that he could offer no retort. He slid to a despondent sitting posture upon the door sill and gazed wretchedly upon the ground, while his companion went to replenish the licorice water at the hydrant—enfeebling the potency of the liquor no doubt, but making up for that in quantity.

"Your mother goin' with you to the cotillon?" asked Sam when he returned.

"No. She's goin' to meet me there. She's goin' somewhere first."

"So's mine," said Sam. "I'll come by for you."

"All right."

"I better go before long. Noon whistles been blowin'."

"All right," Penrod repeated dully.

Sam turned to go, but paused. A new straw hat was peregrinating along the fence near the two boys. This hat belonged to someone passing upon the sidewalk of the cross-street; and the someone was Maurice Levy. Even as they stared, he halted and regarded them over the fence with two small, dark eyes.

Fate had brought about this moment and this confrontation.

CHAPTER XIV
MAURICE LEVY'S CONSTITUTION

"Lo, Sam!" said Maurice cautiously. "What you doin'?"

Penrod at that instant had a singular experience—an intellectual shock like a flash of fire in the brain. Sitting in darkness, a great light flooded him with wild brilliance. He gasped!

"What you doin'?" repeated Mr. Levy.

Penrod sprang to his feet, seized the licorice bottle, shook it with stoppering thumb, and took a long drink with histrionic unction.

"What you doin'?" asked Maurice for the third time, Sam Williams not having decided upon a reply.

It was Penrod who answered.

"Drinkin' lickrish water," he said simply, and wiped his mouth with such delicious enjoyment that Sam's jaded thirst was instantly stimulated. He took the bottle eagerly from Penrod.

"A-a-h!" exclaimed Penrod, smacking his lips. "That was a good un!"

The eyes above the fence glistened.

"Ask him if he don't want some," Penrod whispered urgently. "Quit drinkin' it! It's no good any more. Ask him!"

"What for?" demanded the practical Sam.

"Go on and ask him!" whispered Penrod fiercely.

"Say, M'rice!" Sam called, waving the bottle. "Want some?"

"Bring it here!" Mr. Levy requested.

"Come on over and get some," returned Sam, being prompted.

"I can't. Penrod Schofield's after me."

"No, I'm not," said Penrod reassuringly. "I won't touch you, M'rice. I made up with you yesterday afternoon—don't you remember? You're all right with me, M'rice."

Maurice looked undecided. But Penrod had the delectable bottle again, and tilting it above his lips, affected to let the cool liquid purl enrichingly into him, while with his right hand he stroked his middle facade ineffably. Maurice's mouth watered.

"Here!" cried Sam, stirred again by the superb manifestations of his friend. "Gimme that!"

Penrod brought the bottle down, surprisingly full after so much gusto, but withheld it from Sam; and the two scuffled for its possession. Nothing in the world could have so worked upon the desire of the yearning observer beyond the fence.

"Honest, Penrod—you ain't goin' to touch me if I come in your yard?" he called. "Honest?"

"Cross my heart!" answered Penrod, holding the bottle away from Sam. "And we'll let you drink all you want."

Maurice hastily climbed the fence, and while he was thus occupied Mr. Samuel Williams received a great enlightenment. With startling rapidity Penrod, standing just outside the storeroom door, extended his arm within the room, deposited the licorice water upon the counter of the drug store, seized in its stead the bottle of smallpox medicine, and extended it cordially toward the advancing Maurice.

Genius is like that—great, simple, broad strokes!

Dazzled, Mr. Samuel Williams leaned against the wall. He had the sensations of one who comes suddenly into the presence of a chef-d'oeuvre. Perhaps his first coherent thought was that almost universal one on such huge occasions: "Why couldn't *I* have done that!"

Sam might have been even more dazzled had he guessed that he figured not altogether as a spectator in the sweeping and magnificent conception of the new Talleyrand. Sam had no partner for the cotillon. If Maurice was to be absent from that festivity—as it began to seem he might be—Penrod needed a male friend to take care of Miss Rennsdale and he believed he saw his way to compel Mr. Williams to be that male friend. For this he relied largely upon the prospective conduct of Miss Rennsdale when he should get the matter before her—he was inclined to believe she would favour the exchange. As for Talleyrand Penrod himself, he was going to dance that cotillon with Marjorie Jones!

"You can have all you can drink at one pull, M'rice," said Penrod kindly.

"You said I could have all I want!" protested Maurice, reaching for the bottle.

"No, I didn't," returned Penrod quickly, holding it away from the eager hand.

"He did, too! Didn't he, Sam?"

Sam could not reply; his eyes, fixed upon the bottle, protruded strangely.

"You heard him—didn't you, Sam?"

"Well, if I did say it I didn't mean it!" said Penrod hastily, quoting from one of the authorities. "Looky here, M'rice," he continued, assuming a more placative and reasoning tone, "that wouldn't be fair to us. I guess we want some of our own lickrish water, don't we? The bottle ain't much over two-thirds full anyway. What I meant was, you can have all you can drink at one pull."

"How do you mean?"

"Why, this way: you can gulp all you want, so long as you keep swallering; but you can't take the bottle out of your mouth and commence again. Soon's you quit swallering it's Sam's turn."

"No; you can have next, Penrod," said Sam.

"Well, anyway, I mean M'rice has to give the bottle up the minute he stops swallering."

Craft appeared upon the face of Maurice, like a poster pasted on a wall.

"I can drink so long I don't stop swallering?"

"Yes; that's it."

"All right!" he cried. "Gimme the bottle!"

And Penrod placed it in his hand.

"You promise to let me drink until I quit swallering?" Maurice insisted.

"Yes!" said both boys together.

With that, Maurice placed the bottle to his lips and began to drink. Penrod and Sam leaned forward in breathless excitement. They had feared Maurice might smell the contents of the bottle; but that danger was past—this was the crucial moment. Their fondest hope was that he would make his first swallow a voracious one—it was impossible to imagine a second. They expected one big, gulping swallow and then an explosion, with fountain effects.

Little they knew the mettle of their man! Maurice swallowed once; he swallowed twice—and thrice—and he continued to swallow! No Adam's apple was sculptured on that juvenile throat, but the internal progress of the liquid was not a whit the less visible. His eyes gleamed with cunning and malicious triumph, sidewise, at the stunned conspirators; he was fulfilling the conditions of the draught, not once breaking the thread of that marvelous swallering.

His audience stood petrified. Already Maurice had swallowed more than they had given Duke and still the liquor receded in the uplifted bottle! And now the clear glass gleamed above the dark contents full half the vessel's length—and Maurice went on drinking! Slowly the clear glass increased in its dimensions—slowly the dark diminished.

Sam Williams made a horrified movement to check him—but Maurice protested passionately with his disengaged arm, and made vehement vocal noises reminful of the contract; whereupon

Sam desisted and watched the continuing performance in a state of grisly fascination.

Maurice drank it all! He drained the last drop and threw the bottle in the air, uttering loud ejaculations of triumph and satisfaction.

"Hah!" he cried, blowing out his cheeks, inflating his chest, squaring his shoulders, patting his stomach, and wiping his mouth contentedly. "Hah! Aha! Waha! Wafwah! But that was good!"

The two boys stood looking at him in stupor.

"Well, I gotta say this," said Maurice graciously: "You stuck to your bargain all right and treated me fair."

Stricken with a sudden horrible suspicion, Penrod entered the storeroom in one stride and lifted the bottle of licorice water to his nose—then to his lips. It was weak, but good; he had made no mistake. And Maurice had really drained—to the dregs—the bottle of old hair tonics, dead catsups, syrups of undesirable preserves, condemned extracts of vanilla and lemon, decayed chocolate, ex-essence of beef, mixed dental preparations, aromatic spirits of ammonia, spirits of nitre, alcohol, arnica, quinine, ipecac, sal volatile, nux vomica and licorice water— with traces of arsenic, belladonna and strychnine.

Penrod put the licorice water out of sight and turned to face the others. Maurice was seating himself on a box just outside the door and had taken a package of cigarettes from his pocket.

"Nobody can see me from here, can they?" he said, striking a match. "You fellers smoke?"

"No," said Sam, staring at him haggardly.

"No," said Penrod in a whisper.

Maurice lit his cigarette and puffed showily.

"Well, sir," he remarked, "you fellers are certainly square—I gotta say that

much. Honest, Penrod, I thought you was after me! I did think so," he added sunnily; "but now I guess you like me, or else you wouldn't of stuck to it about lettin' me drink it all if I kept on swallering."

He chatted on with complete geniality, smoking his cigarette in content. And as he ran from one topic to another his hearers stared at him in a kind of torpor. Never once did they exchange a glance with each other; their eyes were frozen to Maurice. The cheerful conversationalist made it evident that he was not without gratitude.

"Well," he said as he finished his cigarette and rose to go, "you fellers have treated me nice and some day you come over to my yard; I'd like to run with you fellers. You're the kind of fellers I like."

Penrod's jaw fell; Sam's mouth had been open all the time. Neither spoke.

"I gotta go," observed Maurice, consulting a handsome watch. "Gotta get dressed for the cotillon right after lunch. Come on, Sam. Don't you have to go, too?"

Sam nodded dazedly.

"Well, good-bye, Penrod," said Maurice cordially. "I'm glad you like me all right. Come on, Sam."

Penrod leaned against the doorpost and with fixed and glazing eyes watched the departure of his two visitors. Maurice was talking volubly, with much gesticulation, as they went; but Sam walked mechanically and in silence, staring at his brisk companion and keeping at a little distance from him.

They passed from sight, Maurice still conversing gayly—and Penrod slowly betook himself into the house, his head bowed upon his chest.

Some three hours later, Mr. Samuel Williams, waxen clean and in sweet raiment, made his reappearance in Penrod's yard, yodelling a code-signal to summon forth his friend. He yodelled loud, long, and frequently, finally securing a faint response from the upper air.

"Where are you?" shouted Mr. Williams, his roving glance searching ambient heights. Another low-spirited yodel reaching his ear, he perceived the head and shoulders of his friend projecting above the roofridge of the stable. The rest of Penrod's body was concealed from view, reposing upon the opposite slant of the gable and precariously secured by the crooking of his elbows over the ridge.

"Yay! What you doin' up there?"

"Nothin'."

"You better be careful!" Sam called. "You'll slide off and fall down in the alley if you don't look out. I come pert' near it last time we was up there. Come on down! Ain't you goin' to the cotillon?"

Penrod made no reply. Sam came nearer.

"Say," he called up in a guarded voice, "I went to our telephone a while ago and ast him how he was feelin', and he said he felt fine!"

"So did I," said Penrod. "He told me he felt bully!"

Sam thrust his hands in his pockets and brooded. The opening of the kitchen door caused a diversion. It was Della.

"Mister Penrod," she bellowed forthwith, "come ahn down fr'm up there! Y'r mamma's at the dancin' class waitin' fer ye, an' she's telephoned me they're goin' to begin—an' what's the matter with ye? Come ahn down fr'm up there!"

"Come on!" urged Sam. "We'll be late. There go Maurice and Marjorie now."

A glittering car spun by, disclosing briefly a genre picture of Marjorie Jones in pink, supporting a monstrous sheaf of American Beauty roses. Maurice, sitting shining and joyous beside her, saw both boys and waved them a hearty greeting as the car turned the corner.

Penrod uttered some muffled words and then waved both arms—either in response or as an expression of his condition of mind; it may have been a gesture of despair. How much intention there was in this act—obviously so rash, considering the position he occupied—it is impossible to say. Undeniably there must remain a suspicion of deliberate purpose.

Della screamed and Sam shouted. Penrod had disappeared from view.

The delayed dance was about to begin a most uneven cotillon when Samuel Williams arrived.

Mrs. Schofield hurriedly left the ballroom; while Miss Rennsdale, flushing with sudden happiness, curtsied profoundly to Professor Bartet and obtained his attention.

"I have told you fifty times," he informed her passionately ere she spoke, "I cannot make no such changes. If your partner comes you have to dance with him. You are going to drive me crazy, sure! What is it? What now? What you want?"

The damsel curtsied again and handed him the following communication, addressed to herself:

"Dear madam Please excuse me from dancing the cotilon with you this afternoon as I have fell off the barn

"Sincerly yours

"PENROD SCHOFIELD."

TO BE CONTINUED IN LITERARY OUTLAW #5

BLACK CAT

---HECTIC LEAD-SLINGING ERA OF THE WILD WEST IS NO MORE--- THE BADMEN OF THE BAD LANDS HAVE SLIPPED OFF INTO THE LONG SLEEP·· BUT HOLLYWOOD WITH ITS MAKE-BELIEVE BRINGS GRIM REALITY TO A SLUMBERING TEXAS TOWN AND STARS THE BLACK CAT IN A DANGERFUL DRAMA OF MOB FURY AND THE

"Banker's Holiday"

LEE ELIAS

READY! ·· HOLLYWOOD HITS WESTERVILLE! FILMING OF GREATEST WESTERN THRILLER MAKES TOWN HISTORY!

THANK YOU, MR. RODGERS FOR ALLOWING US THE FREE USE OF YOUR BANK FOR OUR FILM SEQUENCE!

GLAD TO HELP, MR. DE PILLE! I'VE ARRANGED THE DETAILS WITH THE COUNTERFEIT MONEY!

WHAT A LOVELY TOWN FOR OUR GREAT FILM!

MAIN STREET -- A BEDLAM OF COLOR AND CLAMOR AS THE MAGIC OF MOVIE-MAKING RECREATES THE OLD TIME WEST --
WESTERVILLE BANK & TRUST
BANK
BANK

BANK PRESIDENT RODGERS GIVES LAST MINUTE INSTRUCTIONS --
YOU'VE BEEN A BANK TELLER FOR EIGHT YEARS, WILLIAMS, HOW DOES IT FEEL TO PLAY BANK ROBBER?
I'M A LITTLE SCAIRT! NEVUH RECKONED AH'D PLAY A MOVIE ROLE!

A SOMBER CHORD OF TREACHERY -- OUTSIDE THE BANK -- STACCATO WHISPERS
GIT IT STRAIGHT NAOW -- I GRAB THE DOUGH AND GIT AWAY ON HORSE-BACK -- HAVE THE CAR DOWN AT THE END OF MAIN STREET WITH THE MOTOR RUNNIN'!
GOTCHA, BOSS!

WILLIAMS, KEEP THAT ACTION FAST MOVING! LINDA DEAR, TURN THAT LOVELY FACE TOWARD THE CAMERA -- PLACES! ACTION!
MR. DE PILLE

CAMERA! LENSES FOCUS AND MACHINERY CLICKS AS A DANGEROUS DESPERADO OF THE OLD WEST LIVES AGAIN ---
GIT YOAH HANDS UP, JESSE JAMESON!
OUT'VE MY WAY, GEL! YOU'RE TOO PURTY TO DIE!

NO ONE CAN BEAT JESSIE TO THE DRAW, GEL!
OUCH! MY HAND ---
2

CUT! FINE ACTION! WHERE THE DEUCE IS HE RIDING TO ANYWAY?
THAT'S OVER! HE MUST NEED THE EXERCISE!
EVEN IF THIS IS THE BIGGEST PRODUCTION OF THE YEAR, IT'S NO STORY FOR A REAL NEWSPAPER-MAN!
CHEER UP, RICK-- LET'S STROLL DOWN TO THE GENERAL STORE FOR A SODA AND SOME LOCAL COLOR!
GENERAL STORE--WHERE TOWNSFOLK GATHER TO DISCUSS EVERYTHING FROM FERTILIZER TO FARMER FEUDS---
BUT AH TELLS YUH, LIZZIE, THIS HEAH IS COUNTERFEIT MONEY! AH CAIN'T ACCEPT IT!
IT JEST CAIN'T BE! AH GOT F'M THE BANK! BEN RODGERS WOULD NEVER 'LOW SECH A THING--
THIS IS PHONY ALL RIGHT--SOMETHING'S WRONG SOME-WHERE!
HURRY, RICK! LET'S HAVE A TALK WITH THE BANKER!
BANKER'S NIGHTMARE!--PHONEY MONEY STARTS REAL PANIC!--
IT'S COUNTER-FEIT!
YA CAIN'T CHEAT US!
NO! NO! IT CAN'T BE! WILLIAMS TOOK THE-- WHERE IS WILLIAMS?
SO THAT'S WHY WILLIAMS KEPT RIDING OUT OF TOWN! TELLER TURNS YELLER!
NOT SO FUNNY, RICK! SOME-ONE BETTER TRAIL WILLIAMS!

THE BANK IS CLOSED! IT'S A HOLIDAY! DON'T WORRY ABOUT YOUR MONEY--IT'S SAFE INSIDE THE VAULT!
YOU GUYS GET SOME HORSES! WE'LL TRAIL THAT CROOK! WHAT A STORY! YOWEE!!
SEE YOU ALL LATER--

FROM GLAMOROUS MOVIE STAR TO BLACK CAT, QUEEN OF THE NIGHT--ON THE PROWL---
SOMEHOW THINGS DON'T ADD UP--PERHAPS THE BANK WILL HELP MY FIGURING---

BLACK CAT PICKS A LOCK AND SLITHERS CAUTIOUSLY ACROSS THE SHINY FLOOR OF THE HUSHED BUILDING--

THE VAULT IS OPEN! BETTER HAVE A LOOK--
TELLER

HEAVY MECHANISM WHIRS SOFTLY AS BLACK CAT OPENS THE MIGHTY VAULT DOOR---
WHAT HAVE WE HERE?

BURNING CIGARETTE--SOMEONE WAS HERE A FEW MINUTES AGO!
4

SOMEONE'S COMING NOW!
LA-LA-LA... THE BEST PLACE FOR MONEY IS IN THE BANK -- LA-- LA-LA
HELLO-O, YOU BIG, BAD, BOLD BANK ROBBER --
HOLY COW! WHAT ARE -- WHO (SPLUTTER) -- WHERE'S ...
I GUESS THIS IS WHAT YOU'RE AFTER, YA FEMALE VIPER!
OOF! THANKS, YOU SMALL TIME THIEF!
NOW I'M AGONNA BEAT YA TO A PULP -- DAME OR NO DAME!
WILLIAMS CHARGES WITH THE FEROCITY OF A TRAPPED TIGER -- BUT BLACK CAT IS READY, WILLING AND --
I TAKE YOU BY THE HAND -- TRA-LA --
WHUT IN TARNASHUN!
5

ABLE! A DEFT TWIST OF THE WRIST AND WILLIAMS IS HELPLESS IN THE STEEL HANDS OF THE MISTRESS OF JUDO ···
YER BREAKIN' MAH AHM! AIEE-EE

NOW 'ITTLE GIRL TAKES BIG BAD MANS TO SHERIFF!
PULLEEZE DOAN BREAK IT! I'LL GO QUIETLY!
LET HIM GO BLACK CAT OR YOU'LL BE A DEAD KITTEN!

BLACK CAT DRAWS A LOSING HAND IN THE GAME OF GREED ···
I KNOW WHO YOU ARE, MR. MONEY BAGS!
YOU'LL NEVER LIVE TO TELL ANYONE! GET THE DOUGH, WILLIAMS-- WE'RE LEAVING!

HOUDINI COULDN'T GET OUT OF THERE·· IT'S AIRTIGHT AND SHE'LL BE DEAD BEFORE MORNING WHEN THE LOCK AUTOMATICALLY OPENS ···
IT SERVES THAT SHE-DEVIL RIGHT!

BUT··TROUBLE IS BREWING IN QUIET WESTERVILLE--ANGRY CITIZENS JAM THE GENERAL STORE ···
HOW DO WE KNOW THAT OUR MONEY IS SAFE?
WE DON'T! LET'S FIND OUT!
LET'S OPEN THE BANK!

BREAK DOWN THE DOOR!
BLOW UP THE VAULT!
WE WANT OUR MONEY!
WHERE'S RODGERS?
WESTERVILLE BANK
TRUST CO
B. RODGERS
PRESIDENT

GO HOME! YOUR MONEY IS SAFE IN THE VAULT!
OPEN THE VAULT!
SHOW US THE CASH... UNLESS YER AFEARED!
WESTERVILLE BANK & TRUST CO.
ALL RIGHT--YOU WIN! I'LL OPEN THE VAULT AND SHOW YOU!
HOORAY FOR RODGERS!
ONLY THE FAINTEST FLICKER OF LIFE REMAINS IN THE AIR-STARVED BODY OF THE BLACK CAT···
RODGERS TWIRLS THE VAULT LOCK TUMBLERS AND SWINGS THE DOOR···
JUMPING CATFISH-- IT'S THE--
SHE'S DAID!
THE MONEY'S GONE!
BLACK CAT STOLE YOUR LIFES' SAVINGS! HER PARTNER IS PROBABLY ON HIS WAY OUT OF THE COUNTRY NOW!
STILL HELPLESS, THE BLACK CAT FALLS PREY TO THE MOUNTING FRENZY OF THE LAWLESS MOB!
TO HANGMAN'S HOLLOW WITH HER!
LYNCH HER!
STEAL A POOR WIDDER'S SAVINGS-- WE'LL SHOW YA!
7

RICK, RETURNING WITH THE POSSE MEETS UP WITH THE MOB AND---
WHY--THAT'S BLACK CAT THEY'VE GOT THERE!

TAKE THIS, LUMMOX! WHERE'D YOU THINK YOU WERE TAKING MY BLACK CAT?
SHE STOLE OUR SAVINGS!
GOOD OLE RICK-- CAME IN THE NICK!

AT LAST! THOUGHT DESTROYING COBWEBS VANISH AND BLACK CAT FLASHES INTO MOTION ---
GET BACK, YOU FOOLS! THERE'S YOUR REAL BLACK-HEARTED BANK ROBBER!

PRESIDENT RODGERS--YOU SUBSTITUTED REAL MONEY FOR THE COUNTERFEIT FOR WILLIAMS--BUT YOU WANTED ALL THE MONEY IN THE BANK--SO YOU ARRANGED FOR WILLIAMS TO COME BACK TO THE BANK AND HELP YOU LUG AWAY THE REST OF THE MONEY--THEN YOU WERE GOING INTO BANKRUPTCY AND---

THEN YOU WERE GOING TO LEAVE THE COUNTRY WITH WILLIAMS--HERE ARE YOUR PLANE TICKETS TO BOLIVIA--AND THE MASK YOU WORE WHEN YOU LOCKED ME IN THE VAULT TO DIE!!
I CONFESS-- I'LL RETURN THE MONEY---

ANTICLIMAX! FANATICAL WILLIAMS ENTERS THE SCENE IN A LAST DITCH ATTEMPT TO RESCUE HIS EVIL ACCOMPLICE!!
I'LL SAVE YOU, BOSS! OWW!
DUCK, RICK! JESSE JAMESON TAUGHT ME THIS!
8

> "WE ALL KNOW THAT SOMETHING IS ETERNAL. AND IT AIN'T HOUSES AND IT AIN'T NAMES, AND IT AIN'T EARTH, AND IT AIN'T EVEN THE STARS ... EVERYBODY KNOWS IN THEIR BONES THAT SOMETHING IS ETERNAL, AND THAT SOMETHING HAS TO DO WITH HUMAN BEINGS. ALL THE GREATEST PEOPLE EVER LIVED HAVE BEEN TELLING US THAT FOR FIVE THOUSAND YEARS AND YET YOU'D BE SURPRISED HOW PEOPLE ARE ALWAYS LOSING HOLD OF IT. THERE'S SOMETHING WAY DOWN DEEP THAT'S ETERNAL ABOUT EVERY HUMAN BEING."

— THORNTON WILDER
OUR TOWN

RED SHADOWS

BY ROBERT E. HOWARD

1. THE COMING OF SOLOMON

THE MOONLIGHT SHIMMERED HAZILY, making silvery mists of illusion among the shadowy trees. A faint breeze whispered down the valley, bearing a shadow that was not of the moon-mist. A faint scent of smoke was apparent.

The man whose long, swinging strides, unhurried yet unswerving, had carried him for many a mile since sunrise, stopped suddenly. A movement in the trees had caught his attention, and he moved silently toward the shadows, a hand resting lightly on the hilt of his long, slim rapier.

Warily he advanced, his eyes striving to pierce the darkness that brooded under the trees. This was a wild and menacing country; death might be lurking under those trees. Then his hand fell away from the hilt and he leaned forward. Death indeed was there, but not in such shape as might cause him fear.

"The fires of Hades!" he murmured. "A girl! What has harmed you, child? Be not afraid of me."

The girl looked up at him, her face like a dim white rose in the dark.

"You—who are—you?" her words came in gasps.

"Naught but a wanderer, a landless man, but a friend to all in need." The gentle voice sounded somehow incongruous, coming from the man.

The girl sought to prop herself up on her elbow, and instantly he knelt and raised her to a sitting position, her head resting against his shoulder. His hand touched her breast and came away red and wet.

"Tell me." His voice was soft, soothing, as one speaks to a babe.

"Le Loup," she gasped, her voice swiftly growing weaker. "He and his men—descended upon our village—a mile up the valley. They robbed—slew—burned—"

"That, then, was the smoke I scented," muttered the man. "Go on, child."

"I ran. He, the Wolf, pursued me—and—caught me—" The words died away in a shuddering silence.

"I understand, child. Then—?"

"Then—he—he—stabbed me—with his dagger—oh, blessed saints!—mercy—"

Suddenly the slim form went limp. The man eased her to the earth, and touched her brow lightly.

"Dead!" he muttered.

Slowly he rose, mechanically wiping his hands upon his cloak. A dark scowl had settled on his somber brow. Yet he made no wild, reckless vow, swore no oath by saints or devils.

"Men shall die for this," he said coldly.

2. THE LAIR OF THE WOLF

"YOU ARE A FOOL!" THE WORDS CAME IN A cold snarl that curdled the hearer's blood.

He who had just been named a fool lowered his eyes sullenly without answer.

"You and all the others I lead!" The speaker leaned forward, his fist pounding emphasis on the rude table between them. He was a tall, rangy-built man, supple as a leopard and with a lean, cruel, predatory face. His eyes danced and glittered with a kind of reckless mockery.

The fellow spoken to replied sullenly, "This Solomon Kane is a demon from hell, I tell you."

"Faugh! Dolt! He is a man—who will die from a pistol ball or a sword thrust."

"So thought Jean, Juan and La Costa," answered the other grimly. "Where are they? Ask the mountain wolves that tore the flesh from their dead bones. Where does this Kane hide? We have searched the mountains and the valleys for leagues, and we have found no trace. I tell you, Le Loup, he comes up from hell. I knew no good would come from hanging that friar a moon ago."

The Wolf strummed impatiently upon the table. His keen face, despite lines of wild living and dissipation, was the face of a thinker. The superstitions of his followers affected him not at all.

"Faugh! I say again. The fellow has found some cavern or secret vale of which we do not know where he hides in the day."

"And at night he sallies forth and slays us," gloomily commented the other. "He hunts us down as a wolf hunts deer—by God, Le Loup, you name yourself Wolf but I think you have met at last a fiercer and more crafty wolf than yourself! The first we know of this man is when we find Jean, the most desperate bandit unhung, nailed to a tree with his own dagger through his breast, and the letters S. L. K. carved upon his dead cheeks. Then the Spaniard Juan is struck down, and after we find him he lives long enough to tell us that the slayer is an Englishman, Solomon Kane, who has sworn to destroy our entire band! What then? La Costa, a swordsman second only to yourself, goes forth swearing to meet this Kane. By the demons of perdition, it seems he met him! For we found his sword-pierced corpse upon a cliff. What now? Are we all to fall before this English fiend?"

"True, our best men have been done to death by him," mused the bandit chief. "Soon the rest return from that little trip to the hermit's; then we shall see. Kane can not hide forever. Then—ha, what was that?"

The two turned swiftly as a shadow fell across the table. Into the entrance of the cave that formed the bandit lair, a man staggered. His eyes were wide and staring; he reeled on buckling legs, and a dark red stain dyed his tunic. He came a few tottering steps forward, then pitched across the table, sliding off onto the floor.

"Hell's devils!" cursed the Wolf, hauling him upright and propping him in a chair. "Where are the rest, curse you?"

"Dead! All dead!"

"How? Satan's curses on you, speak!" The Wolf shook the man savagely, the other bandit gazing on in wide-eyed horror.

"We reached the hermit's hut just as the moon rose," the man muttered. "I stayed outside—to watch—the others went in—to torture the hermit—to make him reveal—the hiding-place—of his gold."

"Yes, yes! Then what?" The Wolf was raging with impatience.

"Then the world turned red—the hut went up in a roar and a red rain flooded the valley—through it I saw—the hermit and a tall man clad all in black—coming from the trees—"

"Solomon Kane!" gasped the bandit. "I knew it! I—"

"Silence, fool!" snarled the chief. "Go on!"

"I fled—Kane pursued—wounded me—but I outran—him—got—here—first—"

The man slumped forward on the table.

"Saints and devils!" raged the Wolf. "What does he look like, this Kane?"

"Like—Satan—"

The voice trailed off in silence. The dead man slid from the table to lie in a red heap upon the floor.

"Like Satan!" babbled the other bandit. "I told you! 'Tis the Horned One himself! I tell you—"

He ceased as a frightened face peered in at the cave entrance.

"Kane?"

"Aye." The Wolf was too much at sea to lie. "Keep close watch, La Mon; in a moment the Rat and I will join you."

The face withdrew and Le Loup turned to the other.

"This ends the band," said he. "You, I, and that thief La Mon are all that are left. What would you suggest?"

The Rat's pallid lips barely formed the word: "Flight!"

"You are right. Let us take the gems and gold from the chests and flee, using the secret passageway."

"And La Mon?"

"He can watch until we are ready to flee. Then—why divide the treasure three ways?"

A faint smile touched the Rat's malevolent features. Then a sudden thought smote him.

"He," indicating the corpse on the floor, "said, 'I got here first.' Does that mean Kane was pursuing him here?" And as the Wolf nodded impatiently the other turned to the chests with chattering haste.

The flickering candle on the rough table lighted up a strange and wild scene. The light, uncertain and dancing, gleamed redly in the slowly widening lake of blood in which the dead man lay; it danced upon the heaps of gems and coins emptied hastily upon the floor from the brass-bound chests that ranged the walls; and it glittered in the eyes of the Wolf with the same gleam which sparkled from his sheathed dagger.

The chests were empty, their treasure lying in a shimmering mass upon the blood-stained floor. The Wolf stopped and listened. Outside was silence. There was no moon, and Le Loup's keen imagination pictured the dark slayer, Solomon Kane, gliding through the blackness, a shadow among shadows. He grinned crookedly; this time the Englishman would be foiled.

"There is a chest yet unopened," said he, pointing.

The Rat, with a muttered exclamation of surprise, bent over the chest indicated. With a single, catlike motion, the Wolf sprang upon him, sheathing his dagger to the hilt in the Rat's back, between the shoulders. The Rat sagged to the floor without a sound.

"He sheathed his dagger to the hilt in the Rat's back."

"Why divide the treasure two ways?" murmured Le Loup, wiping his blade upon the dead man's doublet. "Now for La Mon."

He stepped toward the door; then stopped and shrank back.

At first he thought that it was the shadow of a man who stood in the entrance; then he saw that it was a man himself, though so dark and still he stood that a fantastic semblance of shadow was lent him by the guttering candle.

A tall man, as tall as Le Loup he was, clad in black from head to foot, in plain, close-fitting garments that somehow suited the somber face. Long arms and broad shoulders betokened the swordsman, as plainly as the long rapier in his hand. The features of the man were saturnine and gloomy. A kind of dark pallor lent him a ghostly appearance in the uncertain light, an effect heightened by the satanic darkness of his lowering brows. Eyes, large, deep-set and unblinking, fixed their gaze upon the bandit, and looking into them, Le Loup was unable to decide what color they were. Strangely, the mephistophelean trend of the lower features was offset by a high, broad forehead, though this was partly hidden by a featherless hat.

That forehead marked the dreamer, the idealist, the introvert, just as the eyes and the thin, straight nose betrayed the fanatic. An observer would have been struck by the eyes of the two men who stood there, facing each other. Eyes of both betokened untold deeps of power, but there the resemblance ceased.

The eyes of the bandit were hard, almost opaque, with a curious scintillant shallowness that reflected a thousand changing lights and gleams, like some strange gem; there was mockery in those eyes, cruelty and recklessness.

The eyes of the man in black, on the other hand, deep-set and staring from under prominent brows, were cold but deep; gazing into them, one had the impression of looking into countless fathoms of ice.

Now the eyes clashed, and the Wolf, who was used to being feared, felt a strange coolness on his spine. The sensation was new to him—a new thrill to one who lived for thrills, and he laughed suddenly.

"You are Solomon Kane, I suppose?" he asked, managing to make his question sound politely incurious.

"I am Solomon Kane." The voice was resonant and powerful. "Are you prepared to meet your God?"

"Why, *Monsieur*," Le Loup answered, bowing, "I assure you I am as ready as I ever will be. I might ask *Monsieur* the same question."

"No doubt I stated my inquiry wrongly," Kane said grimly. "I will change it: Are you prepared to meet your master, the Devil?"

"As to that, *Monsieur*"—Le Loup examined his finger nails with elaborate unconcern—"I must say that I can at present render a most satisfactory account to his Horned Excellency, though really I have no intention of so doing—for a while at least."

Le Loup did not wonder as to the fate of La Mon; Kane's presence in the cave was sufficient answer that did not need the trace of blood on his rapier to verify it.

"What I wish to know, *Monsieur*," said the bandit, "is why in the Devil's name have you harassed my band as you have, and how did you destroy that last set of fools?"

"Your last question is easily answered, sir," Kane replied. "I myself had the tale spread that the hermit possessed a store of gold, knowing that would draw your scum as carrion draws vultures. For days and nights I have watched the hut, and tonight, when I saw your villains coming, I warned the hermit, and together we went among the trees back of the hut. Then, when the rogues were inside, I struck flint and steel to the train I had laid, and flame ran through the trees like a red snake until it reached the powder I had placed beneath the hut floor. Then the hut and thirteen sinners went to hell in a great roar of flame and smoke. True, one escaped, but him I had slain in the forest had not I stumbled and fallen upon a broken root, which gave him time to elude me."

«*Monsieur*," said Le Loup with another low bow, "I grant you the admiration I must needs bestow on a brave and shrewd foeman. Yet tell me this: Why have you followed me as a wolf follows deer?"

"Some moons ago," said Kane, his frown becoming more menacing, "you and your fiends raided a small village down the valley. You know the details better than I. There was a girl there, a mere child, who, hoping to escape your lust, fled up the valley; but you, you jackal of hell, you caught her and left her, violated and dying. I found her there, and above her dead form I made up my mind to hunt you down and kill you."

"H'm," mused the Wolf. "Yes, I remember the wench. *Mon Dieu*, so the softer sentiments enter into the affair!

Monsieur, I had not thought you an amorous man; be not jealous, good fellow, there are many more wenches."

"Le Loup, take care!" Kane exclaimed, a terrible menace in his voice, "I have never yet done a man to death by torture, but by God, sir, you tempt me!"

The tone, and more especially the unexpected oath, coming as it did from Kane, slightly sobered Le Loup; his eyes narrowed and his hand moved toward his rapier. The air was tense for an instant; then the Wolf relaxed elaborately.

"Who was the girl?" he asked idly, "Your wife?"

"I never saw her before," answered Kane.

«*Nom d'un nom!*» swore the bandit. "What sort of a man are you, *Monsieur*, who takes up a feud of this sort merely to avenge a wench unknown to you?"

"That, sir, is my own affair; it is sufficient that I do so."

Kane could not have explained, even to himself, nor did he ever seek an explanation within himself. A true fanatic, his promptings were reasons enough for his actions.

"You are right, *Monsieur*." Le Loup was sparring now for time; casually he edged backward inch by inch, with such consummate acting skill that he aroused no suspicion even in the hawk who watched him. "*Monsieur*," said he, "possibly you will say that you are merely a noble cavalier, wandering about like a true Galahad, protecting the weaker; but you and I know different. There on the floor is the equivalent to an emperor's ransom. Let us divide it peaceably; then if you like not my company, why—*nom d'un nom!*—we can go our separate ways."

Kane leaned forward, a terrible brooding threat growing in his cold eyes. He seemed like a great condor about to launch himself upon his victim.

"Sir, do you assume me to be as great a villain as yourself?"

Suddenly Le Loup threw back his head, his eyes dancing and leaping with a wild mockery and a kind of insane recklessness. His shout of laughter sent the echoes flying.

"Gods of hell! No, you fool, I do not class you with myself! *Mon Dieu*, Monsieur Kane, you have a task indeed if you intend to avenge all the wenches who have known my favors!"

"Shades of death! Shall I waste time in parleying with this base scoundrel!" Kane snarled in a voice suddenly blood-thirsting, and his lean frame flashed forward like a bent bow suddenly released.

At the same instant Le Loup with a wild laugh bounded backward with a movement as swift as Kane's. His timing was perfect; his back-flung hands struck the table and hurled it aside, plunging the cave into darkness as the candle toppled and went out.

Kane's rapier sang like an arrow in the dark as he thrust blindly and ferociously.

«*Adieu*, Monsieur Galahad!" The taunt came from somewhere in front of him, but Kane, plunging toward the sound with the savage fury of baffled wrath, caromed against a blank wall that did not yield to his blow. From somewhere seemed to come an echo of a mocking laugh.

Kane whirled, eyes fixed on the dimly outlined entrance, thinking his foe would try to slip past him and out of the cave; but no form bulked there, and when his groping hands found the candle and lighted it, the cave was empty, save for himself and the dead men on the floor.

3. THE CHANT OF THE DRUMS

Across the dusky waters the whisper came: boom, boom, boom!—a sullen reiteration. Far away and more faintly sounded a whisper of different timbre: thrum, throom, thrum! Back and forth went the vibrations as the throbbing drums spoke to each other. What tales did they carry? What monstrous secrets whispered across the sullen, shadowy reaches of the unmapped jungle?

"This, you are sure, is the bay where the Spanish ship put in?"

"Yes, *Senhor*, the negro swears this is the bay where the white man left the ship alone and went into the jungle."

Kane nodded grimly.

"Then put me ashore here, alone. Wait seven days; then if I have not returned and if you have no word of me, set sail wherever you will."

"Yes, *Senhor*."

The waves slapped lazily against the sides of the boat that carried Kane ashore. The village that he sought was on the river bank but set back from the bay shore, the jungle hiding it from sight of the ship.

Kane had adopted what seemed the most hazardous course, that of going ashore by night, for the reason that he knew, if the man he sought were in the village, he would never reach it by day. As it was, he was taking a most desperate chance in daring the nighttime jungle, but all his life he had been used to taking desperate chances. Now he gambled his life upon the slim chance of gaining the negro village under cover of darkness and unknown to the villagers.

At the beach he left the boat with a few muttered commands, and as the rowers put back to the ship which lay anchored some distance out in the bay, he turned and engulfed himself in the blackness of the jungle. Sword in one hand, dagger in the other, he stole forward, seeking to keep pointed in the direction from which the drums still muttered and grumbled.

He went with the stealth and easy movement of a leopard, feeling his way cautiously, every nerve alert and straining,

but the way was not easy. Vines tripped him and slapped him in the face, impeding his progress; he was forced to grope his way between the huge boles of towering trees, and all through the underbrush about him sounded vague and menacing rustlings and shadows of movement. Thrice his foot touched something that moved beneath it and writhed away, and once he glimpsed the baleful glimmer of feline eyes among the trees. They vanished, however, as he advanced.

Thrum, thrum, thrum, came the ceaseless monotone of the drums: war and death (they said); blood and lust; human sacrifice and human feast! The soul of Africa (said the drums); the spirit of the jungle; the chant of the gods of outer darkness, the gods that roar and gibber, the gods men knew when dawns were young, beast-eyed, gaping-mouthed, huge-bellied, bloody-handed, the Black Gods (sang the drums).

All this and more the drums roared and bellowed to Kane as he worked his way through the forest. Somewhere in his soul a responsive chord was smitten and answered. You too are of the night (sang the drums); there is the strength of darkness, the strength of the primitive in you; come back down the ages; let us teach you, let us teach you (chanted the drums).

Kane stepped out of the thick jungle and came upon a plainly defined trail. Beyond, through the trees came the gleam of the village fires, flames glowing through the palisades. Kane walked down the trail swiftly.

He went silently and warily, sword extended in front of him, eyes straining to catch any hint of movement in the darkness ahead, for the trees loomed like sullen giants on each hand; sometimes their great branches intertwined above the trail and he could see only a slight way ahead of him.

Like a dark ghost he moved along the shadowed trail; alertly he stared and harkened; yet no warning came first to him, as a great, vague bulk rose up out of the shadows and struck him down, silently.

4. THE BLACK GOD

THRUM, THRUM, THRUM! SOMEWHERE, with deadening monotony, a cadence was repeated, over and over, bearing out the same theme: "Fool—fool—fool!" Now it was far away, now he could stretch out his hand and almost reach it. Now it merged with the throbbing in his head until the two vibrations were as one: "Fool—fool—fool—fool—"

The fogs faded and vanished. Kane sought to raise his hand to his head, but found that he was bound hand and foot. He lay on the floor of a hut—alone? He twisted about to view the place. No, two eyes glimmered at him from the darkness. Now a form took shape, and Kane, still mazed, believed that he looked on the man who had struck him unconscious. Yet no; this man could never strike such a blow. He was lean, withered and wrinkled. The only thing that seemed alive about him were his eyes, and they seemed like the eyes of a snake.

The man squatted on the floor of the hut, near the doorway, naked save for a loin-cloth and the usual paraphernalia of bracelets, anklets and armlets. Weird fetishes of ivory, bone and hide, animal and human, adorned his arms and legs. Suddenly and unexpectedly he spoke in English.

"Ha, you wake, white man? Why you come here, eh?"

Kane asked the inevitable question, following the habit of the Caucasian.

"You speak my language—how is that?"

The black man grinned.

"I slave—long time, me boy. Me, N'Longa, ju-ju man, me, great fetish. No black man like me! You white man, you hunt brother?"

Kane snarled. "I! Brother! I seek a man, yes."

The negro nodded. "Maybe so you find um, eh?"

"He dies!"

Again the negro grinned. "Me pow'rful ju-ju man," he announced apropos of nothing. He bent closer. "White man you hunt, eyes like a leopard, eh? Yes? Ha! ha! ha! ha! Listen, white man: man-with-eyes-of-a-leopard, he and Chief Songa make pow'rful palaver; they blood brothers now. Say nothing, I help you; you help me, eh?"

"Why should you help me?" asked Kane suspiciously.

The ju-ju man bent closer and whispered, "White man Songa's right-hand man; Songa more pow'rful than N'Longa. White man mighty ju-ju! N'Longa's white brother kill man-with-eyes-of-a-leopard, be blood brother to N'Longa, N'Longa be more pow'rful than Songa; palaver set."

And like a dusky ghost he floated out of the hut so swiftly that Kane was not sure but that the whole affair was a dream.

Without, Kane could see the flare of fires. The drums were still booming, but close at hand the tones merged and mingled, and the impulse-producing vibrations were lost. All seemed a barbaric clamor without rime or reason, yet there was an undertone of mockery there, savage and gloating. "Lies," thought Kane, his mind still swimming, "jungle lies like jungle women that lure a man to his doom."

Two warriors entered the hut—black giants, hideous with paint and armed with crude spears. They lifted the white man and carried him out of the hut. They bore him across an open space, leaned him upright against a post and bound him there. About him, behind him and to the side, a great semicircle of black faces leered and faded in the firelight as the flames leaped and sank. There in front of him loomed a shape hideous and obscene—a black, formless thing, a grotesque parody of the human. Still, brooding, blood-stained, like the formless soul of Africa, the horror, the Black God.

And in front and to each side, upon roughly carven thrones of teakwood, sat two men. He who sat upon the right was a black man, huge, ungainly, a gigantic and unlovely mass of dusky flesh and muscles. Small, hog-like eyes blinked out over sin-marked cheeks; huge, flabby red lips pursed in fleshly haughtiness.

The other—

"Ah, *Monsieur*, we meet again." The speaker was far from being the debonair villain who had taunted Kane in the cavern among the mountains. His clothes were rags; there were more lines in his face; he had sunk lower in the years that had passed. Yet his eyes still gleamed and danced with their old recklessness and his voice held the same mocking timbre.

"The last time I heard that accursed voice," said Kane calmly, "was in a cave, in darkness, whence you fled like a hunted rat."

"Aye, under different conditions," answered Le Loup imperturbably. "What did you do after blundering about like an elephant in the dark?"

Kane hesitated, then: "I left the mountain—"

"By the front entrance? Yes? I might have known you were too stupid to find the secret door. Hoofs of the Devil, had you thrust against the chest with the golden lock, which stood against the wall, the door had opened to you and revealed the secret passageway through which I went."

"I traced you to the nearest port and there took ship and followed you to Italy, where I found you had gone."

"Aye, by the saints, you nearly cornered me in Florence. Ho! ho! ho! I was climbing through a back window while Monsieur Galahad was battering down the front door of the tavern. And had your horse not gone lame, you would have caught up with me on the road to Rome. Again, the ship on which I left Spain had barely put out to sea when Monsieur Galahad rides up to the wharfs. Why have you followed me like this? I do not understand."

"Because you are a rogue whom it is my destiny to kill," answered Kane coldly. He did not understand. All his life he had roamed about the world aiding the weak and fighting oppression, he neither knew nor questioned why. That was his obsession, his driving force of life. Cruelty and tyranny to the weak sent a red blaze of fury, fierce and lasting, through his soul. When the full flame of his hatred was wakened and loosed, there was no rest for him until his vengeance had been fulfilled to the uttermost. If he thought of it at all, he considered himself a fulfiller of God's judgment, a vessel of wrath to be emptied upon the souls of the unrighteous. Yet in the full sense of the word Solomon Kane was not wholly a Puritan, though he thought of himself as such.

Le Loup shrugged his shoulders. "I could understand had I wronged you personally. *Mon Dieu!* I, too, would follow an enemy across the world, but, though I would have joyfully slain and robbed you, I never heard of you until you declared war on me."

Kane was silent, his still fury overcoming him. Though he did not realize it, the Wolf was more than merely an enemy to him; the bandit symbolized, to Kane, all the things against which the Puritan had fought all his life: cruelty, outrage, oppression and tyranny.

Le Loup broke in on his vengeful meditations. "What did you do with the treasure, which—gods of Hades!—took me years to accumulate? Devil take it, I had time only to snatch a handful of coins and trinkets as I ran."

"I took such as I needed to hunt you down. The rest I gave to the villages which you had looted."

"Saints and the devil!" swore Le Loup. "*Monsieur*, you are the greatest fool I have yet met. To throw that vast treasure—by Satan, I rage to think of it in the hands of base peasants, vile villagers! Yet, ho! ho! ho! ho! they will steal, and kill each other for it! That is human nature."

"Yes, damn you!" flamed Kane suddenly, showing that his conscience had not been at rest. "Doubtless they will, being fools. Yet what could I do? Had I left it there, people might have starved and gone naked for lack of it. More, it would have been found, and theft and slaughter would have followed anyway. You are to blame, for had this treasure been left with its rightful owners, no such trouble would have ensued."

The Wolf grinned without reply. Kane not being a profane man, his rare curses had double effect and always startled his hearers, no matter how vicious or hardened they might be.

It was Kane who spoke next. "Why have you fled from me across the world? You do not really fear me."

"No, you are right. Really I do not know; perhaps flight is a habit which is difficult to break. I made my mistake when I did not kill you that night in the mountains. I am sure I could kill you in a fair fight, yet I have never even, ere now, sought to ambush you. Somehow I have not had a liking to meet you, *Monsieur*—a whim of mine, a mere whim. Then—*mon Dieu!*—mayhap I have enjoyed a new sensation—and I had thought that I had exhausted the thrills of life. And then, a man must either be the hunter or the hunted. Until now, *Monsieur*, I was the hunted, but I grew weary of the rôle—I thought I had thrown you off the trail."

"A negro slave, brought from this vicinity, told a Portugal ship captain of a white man who landed from a Spanish ship and went into the jungle. I heard of it and hired the ship, paying the captain to bring me here."

«*Monsieur*, I admire you for your attempt, but you must admire me, too! Alone I came into this village, and alone among savages and cannibals I—with some slight knowledge of the language learned from a slave aboard ship—I gained the confidence of King Songa and supplanted that mummer, N'Longa. I am a braver man than you, *Monsieur*, for I had no ship to retreat to, and a ship is waiting for you."

"I admire your courage," said Kane, "but you are content to rule amongst cannibals—you the blackest soul of them all. I intend to return to my own people when I have slain you."

"Your confidence would be admirable were it not amusing. Ho, Gulka!"

A giant negro stalked into the space between them. He was the hugest man that Kane had ever seen, though he moved with catlike ease and suppleness. His arms and legs were like trees, and the great, sinuous muscles rippled with each motion. His apelike head was set squarely between gigantic shoulders. His great, dusky hands were like the talons of an ape, and his brow slanted back from above bestial eyes. Flat nose and great, thick red lips completed this picture of primitive, lustful savagery.

"That is Gulka, the gorilla-slayer," said Le Loup. "He it was who lay in wait beside the trail and smote you down. You are like a wolf, yourself, Monsieur Kane, but since your ship hove in sight you have been watched by many eyes, and had you had all the powers of a leopard, you had not seen Gulka nor heard him. He hunts the most terrible and crafty of all beasts, in their native forests, far to the north, the beasts-who-walk-like-men—as that one, whom he slew some days since."

Kane, following Le Loup's fingers, made out a curious, manlike thing, dangling from a roof-pole of a hut. A jagged end thrust through the thing's body held it there. Kane could scarcely distinguish its characteristics by the firelight, but there was a weird, humanlike semblance about the hideous, hairy thing.

"A female gorilla that Gulka slew and brought to the village," said Le Loup.

The giant black slouched close to Kane and stared into the white man's eyes. Kane returned his gaze somberly, and presently the negro's eyes dropped sullenly and he slouched back a few paces. The look in the Puritan's grim eyes had pierced the primitive hazes of the gorilla-slayer's soul, and for the first time in his life he felt fear. To throw this off, he tossed a challenging look about; then, with unexpected animalness, he struck his huge chest resoundingly, grinned cavernously and flexed his mighty arms. No one spoke. Primordial bestiality had the stage, and the more highly developed types looked on with various feelings of amusement, tolerance or contempt.

Gulka glanced furtively at Kane to see if the white man was watching him, then with a sudden beastly roar, plunged forward and dragged a man from the semicircle. While the trembling victim screeched for mercy, the giant hurled him upon the crude altar before the shadowy idol. A spear rose and flashed, and the screeching ceased. The Black God looked on, his monstrous features seeming to leer in the flickering firelight. He had drunk; was the Black God pleased with the draft—with the sacrifice?

Gulka stalked back, and stopping before Kane, flourished the bloody spear before the white man's face.

Le Loup laughed. Then suddenly N'Longa appeared. He came from nowhere in particular; suddenly he was standing there, beside the post to which Kane was bound. A lifetime of study of the art of illusion had given the ju-ju man a highly technical knowledge of appearing and disappearing—which after all, consisted only in timing the audience's attention.

He waved Gulka aside with a grand gesture, and the gorilla-man slunk back, apparently to get out of N'Longa's gaze—then with incredible swiftness he turned and struck the ju-ju man a terrific blow upon the side of the head with his open hand. N'Longa went down like a felled ox, and in an instant he had been seized and bound to a post close to Kane. An uncertain murmuring rose from the negroes, which died out as King Songa stared angrily toward them.

Le Loup leaned back upon his throne and laughed uproariously.

"The trail ends here, Monsieur Galahad. That ancient fool thought I did not know of his plotting! I was hiding outside the hut and heard the interesting conversation you two had. Ha! ha! ha! ha! The Black God must drink, *Monsieur*, but I have persuaded Songa to have you two burnt; that will be much more enjoyable, though we shall have to forego the usual feast, I fear. For after the fires are lit about your feet the devil himself could not keep your carcasses from becoming charred frames of bone."

Songa shouted something imperiously, and blacks came bearing wood, which they piled about the feet of N'Longa and Kane. The ju-ju man had recovered consciousness, and he now shouted something in his native language. Again the murmuring arose among the shadowy throng. Songa snarled something in reply.

Kane gazed at the scene almost impersonally. Again, somewhere in his soul, dim primal deeps were stirring, age-old thought memories, veiled in the fogs of lost eons. He had been here before, thought Kane; he knew all this of old—the lurid flames beating back the sullen night, the bestial faces leering expectantly, and the god, the Black God, there in the shadows! Always the Black God, brooding back in the shadows. He had known the shouts, the frenzied chant of the worshipers, back there in the gray dawn of the world, the speech of the bellowing drums, the singing priests, the repellent, inflaming, all-pervading scent of freshly spilt blood. All this have I known, somewhere, sometime, thought Kane; now I am the main actor—

He became aware that someone was speaking to him through the roar of the drums; he had not realized that the drums had begun to boom again. The speaker was N'Longa:

"Me pow'rful ju-ju man! Watch now: I work mighty magic. Songa!" His voice rose in a screech that drowned out the wildly clamoring drums.

Songa grinned at the words N'Longa screamed at him. The chant of the drums now had dropped to a low, sinister monotone and Kane plainly heard Le Loup when he spoke:

"N'Longa says that he will now work that magic which it is death to speak, even. Never before has it been worked in the sight of living men; it is the nameless ju-ju magic. Watch closely, *Monsieur*, possibly we shall be further amused." The Wolf laughed lightly and sardonically.

A black man stooped, applying a torch to the wood about Kane's feet. Tiny jets of flame began to leap up and catch. Another bent to do the same with N'Longa, then hesitated. The ju-ju man sagged in his bonds; his head drooped upon his chest. He seemed dying.

Le Loup leaned forward, cursing, "Feet of the Devil! is the scoundrel about to cheat us of our pleasure of seeing him writhe in the flames?"

The warrior gingerly touched the wizard and said something in his own language.

Le Loup laughed: "He died of fright. A great wizard, by the—"

His voice trailed off suddenly. The drums stopped as if the drummers had fallen dead simultaneously. Silence dropped like a fog upon the village and in the stillness Kane heard only the sharp crackle of the flames whose heat he was beginning to feel.

All eyes were turned upon the dead man upon the altar, *for the corpse had begun to move!*

First a twitching of a hand, then an aimless motion of an arm, a motion which gradually spread over the body and limbs. Slowly, with blind, uncertain gestures, the dead man turned upon his side, the trailing limbs found the earth. Then, horribly like something being born, like some frightful reptilian thing bursting the shell of non-existence, the corpse tottered and reared upright, standing on legs wide apart and stiffly braced, arms still making useless, infantile motions. Utter silence, save somewhere a man's quick breath sounded loud in the stillness.

Kane stared, for the first time in his life smitten speechless and thoughtless. To his Puritan mind this was Satan's hand manifested.

Le Loup sat on his throne, eyes wide and staring, hand still half raised in the careless gesture he was making when frozen into silence by the unbelievable sight. Songa sat beside him, mouth and eyes wide open, fingers making curious jerky motions upon the carved arms of the throne.

Now the corpse was upright, swaying on stiltlike legs, body tilting far back until the sightless eyes seemed to stare straight into the red moon that was just rising over the black jungle. The thing tottered uncertainly in a wide, erratic half-circle, arms flung out grotesquely as if in balance, then swaying about to face the two thrones—and the Black God. A burning twig at Kane's feet cracked like the crash of a cannon in the tense silence. The horror thrust forth a black foot—it took a wavering step—another. Then with stiff, jerky and automatonlike steps, legs straddled far apart, the dead man came toward the two who sat in speechless horror to each side of the Black God.

"Ah-h-h!" from somewhere came the explosive sigh, from that shadowy semicircle where crouched the terror-fascinated worshippers. Straight on stalked the grim specter. Now it was within three strides of the thrones, and Le Loup, faced by fear for the first time in his bloody life, cringed back in his chair; while Songa, with a superhuman effort breaking the chains of horror that held him helpless, shattered the night with a wild scream and, springing to his feet, lifted a spear, shrieking and gibbering in wild menace. Then as the ghastly thing halted not its frightful advance, he hurled the spear with all the power of his great, black muscles, and the spear tore through the dead man's breast with a rending of flesh and bone. Not an instant halted the thing—for the dead die not—and Songa the king stood frozen, arms outstretched as if to fend off the terror.

An instant they stood so, leaping firelight and eery moonlight etching the scene forever in the minds of the beholders. The changeless staring eyes of the corpse looked full into the bulging eyes of Songa, where were reflected all the hells of horror. Then with a jerky motion the arms of the thing went out and up. The dead hands fell on Songa's shoulders. At the first touch, the king seemed to shrink and shrivel, and with a scream that was to haunt the dreams of every watcher through all the rest of time, Songa crumpled and fell, and the dead man reeled stiffly and fell with him. Motionless lay the two at the feet of the Black God, and to Kane's dazed mind it seemed that the idol's great, inhuman eyes were fixed upon them with terrible, still laughter.

"The dead man reeled and fell with him."

At the instant of the king's fall, a great shout went up from the blacks, and Kane, with a clarity lent his subconscious mind by the depths of his hate, looked for Le Loup and saw him spring from his throne and vanish in the darkness. Then vision was blurred by a rush of black figures who swept into the space before the god. Feet knocked aside the blazing brands whose heat Kane had forgotten, and dusky hands freed him; others loosed the wizard's body and laid it upon the earth. Kane dimly understood that the blacks believed this thing to be the work of N'Longa, and that they connected the vengeance of the wizard with himself. He bent, laid a hand on the ju-ju man's shoulder. No doubt of it: he was dead, the flesh was already cold. He glanced at the other corpses. Songa was dead, too, and the thing that had slain him lay now without movement.

Kane started to rise, then halted. Was he dreaming, or did he really feel a sudden warmth in the dead flesh he touched? Mind reeling, he again bent over the wizard's body, and slowly he felt warmness steal over the limbs and the blood begin to flow sluggishly through the veins again.

Then N'Longa opened his eyes and stared up into Kane's, with the blank expression of a new-born babe. Kane watched, flesh crawling, and saw the knowing, reptilian glitter come back, saw the wizard's thick lips part in a wide grin. N'Longa sat up, and a strange chant arose from the negroes.

Kane looked about. The blacks were all kneeling, swaying their bodies to and fro, and in their shouts Kane caught the word, "N'Longa!" repeated over and over in a kind of fearsomely ecstatic refrain of terror and worship. As the wizard rose, they all fell prostrate.

N'Longa nodded, as if in satisfaction.

"Great ju-ju—great fetish, me!" he announced to Kane. "You see? My ghost go out—kill Songa—come back to me! Great magic! Great fetish, me!"

Kane glanced at the Black God looming back in the shadows, at N'Longa, who now flung out his arms toward the idol as if in invocation.

I am everlasting (Kane thought the Black God said); I drink, no matter who rules; chiefs, slayers, wizards, they pass like the ghosts of dead men through the gray jungle; I stand, I rule; I am the soul of the jungle (said the Black God).

Suddenly Kane came back from the illusory mists in which he had been wandering. "The white man! Which way did he flee?"

N'Longa shouted something. A score of dusky hands pointed; from somewhere Kane's rapier was thrust out to him. The fogs faded and vanished; again he was the avenger, the scourge of the unrighteous; with the sudden volcanic speed of a tiger he snatched the sword and was gone.

5. THE END OF THE RED TRAIL

LIMBS AND VINES SLAPPED AGAINST KANE'S face. The oppressive steam of the tropic night rose like mist about him. The moon, now floating high above the jungle, limned the black shadows in its white glow and patterned the jungle floor in grotesque designs. Kane knew not if the man he sought was ahead of him, but broken limbs and trampled underbrush showed that some man had gone that way, some man who fled in haste, nor halted to pick his way. Kane followed these signs unswervingly. Believing in the justice of his vengeance, he did not doubt that the dim beings who rule men's destinies would finally bring him face to face with Le Loup.

Behind him the drums boomed and muttered. What a tale they had to tell this night! of the triumph of N'Longa, the death of the black king, the overthrow of the   white-man-with-eyes-like-a-leopard, and a more darksome tale, a tale to be whispered in low, muttering vibrations: the nameless ju-ju.

Was he dreaming? Kane wondered as he hurried on. Was all this part of some foul magic? He had seen a dead man rise and slay and die again; he had seen a man die and come to life again. Did N'Longa in truth send his ghost, his soul, his life essence forth into the void, dominating a corpse to do his will? Aye, N'Longa died a real death there, bound to the torture stake, and he who lay dead on the altar rose and did as N'Longa would have done had he been free. Then, the unseen force animating the dead man fading, N'Longa had lived again.

Yes, Kane thought, he must admit it as a fact. Somewhere in the darksome reaches of jungle and river, N'Longa had stumbled upon the Secret—the Secret of controlling life and death, of overcoming the shackles and limitations of the flesh. How had this dark wisdom, born in the black and blood-stained shadows of this grim land, been given to the wizard? What sacrifice had been so pleasing to the Black Gods, what ritual so monstrous, as to make them give up the knowledge of this magic? And what thoughtless, timeless journeys had N'Longa taken, when he chose to send his ego, his ghost, through the far, misty countries, reached only by death?

There is wisdom in the shadows (brooded the drums), wisdom and magic; go into the darkness for wisdom; ancient magic shuns the light; we remember the lost ages (whispered the drums), ere man became wise and foolish; we remember the beast gods—the serpent gods and the ape gods and the nameless, the Black

Gods, they who drank blood and whose voices roared through the shadowy hills, who feasted and lusted. The secrets of life and of death are theirs; we remember, we remember (sang the drums).

Kane heard them as he hastened on. The tale they told to the feathered black warriors farther up the river, he could not translate; but they spoke to him in their own way, and that language was deeper, more basic.

The moon, high in the dark blue skies, lighted his way and gave him a clear vision as he came out at last into a glade and saw Le Loup standing there. The Wolf's naked blade was a long gleam of silver in the moon, and he stood with shoulders thrown back, the old, defiant smile still on his face.

"A long trail, *Monsieur*," said he. "It began in the mountains of France; it ends in an African jungle. I have wearied of the game at last, *Monsieur*—and you die. I had not fled from the village, even, save that—I admit it freely—that damnable witchcraft of N'Longa's shook my nerves. More, I saw that the whole tribe would turn against me."

Kane advanced warily, wondering what dim, forgotten tinge of chivalry in the bandit's soul had caused him thus to take his chance in the open. He half suspected treachery, but his keen eyes could detect no shadow of movement in the jungle on either side of the glade.

«*Monsieur*, on guard!" Le Loup's voice was crisp. "Time that we ended this fool's dance about the world. Here we are alone."

The men were now within reach of each other, and Le Loup, in the midst of his sentence, suddenly plunged forward with the speed of light, thrusting viciously. A slower man had died there, but Kane parried and sent his own blade in a silver streak that slit Le Loup's tunic as the Wolf bounded backward. Le Loup admitted the failure of his trick with a wild laugh and

came in with the breath-taking speed and fury of a tiger, his blade making a white fan of steel about him.

Rapier clashed on rapier as the two swordsmen fought. They were fire and ice opposed. Le Loup fought wildly but craftily, leaving no openings, taking advantage of every opportunity. He was a living flame, bounding back, leaping in, feinting, thrusting, warding, striking—laughing like a wild man, taunting and cursing.

Kane's skill was cold, calculating, scintillant. He made no waste movement, no motion not absolutely necessary. He seemed to devote more time and effort toward defense than did Le Loup, yet there was no hesitancy in his attack, and when he thrust, his blade shot out with the speed of a striking snake.

There was little to choose between the men as to height, strength and reach. Le Loup was the swifter by a scant, flashing margin, but Kane's skill reached a finer point of perfection. The Wolf's fencing was fiery, dynamic, like the blast from a furnace. Kane was more steady—less the instinctive, more the thinking fighter, though he, too, was a born slayer, with the co-ordination that only a natural fighter possessed.

Thrust, parry, a feint, a sudden whirl of blades—

"Ha!" the Wolf sent up a shout of ferocious laughter as the blood started from a cut on Kane's cheek. As if the sight drove him to further fury, he attacked like the beast men named him. Kane was forced back before that blood-lusting onslaught, but the Puritan's expression did not alter.

Minutes flew by; the clang and clash of steel did not diminish. Now they stood squarely in the center of the glade, Le Loup untouched, Kane's garments red with the blood that oozed from wounds on cheek, breast, arm and thigh. The Wolf grinned savagely and mockingly in the moonlight, but he had begun to doubt.

His breath came hissing fast and his arm began to weary; who was this man of steel and ice who never seemed to weaken? Le Loup knew that the wounds he had inflicted on Kane were not deep, but even so, the steady flow of blood should have sapped some of the man's strength and speed by this time. But if Kane felt the ebb of his powers, it did not show. His brooding countenance did not change in expression, and he pressed the fight with as much cold fury as at the beginning.

Le Loup felt his might fading, and with one last desperate effort he rallied all his fury and strength into a single plunge. A sudden, unexpected attack too wild and swift for the eye to follow, a dynamic burst of speed and fury no man could have withstood, and Solomon Kane reeled for the first time as he felt cold steel tear through his body. He reeled back, and Le Loup, with a wild shout, plunged after him, his reddened sword free, a gasping taunt on his lips.

Kane's sword, backed by the force of desperation, met Le Loup's in midair; met, held and wrenched. The Wolf's yell of triumph died on his lips as his sword flew singing from his hand.

For a fleeting instant he stopped short, arms flung wide as a crucifix, and Kane heard his wild, mocking laughter peal forth for the last time, as the Englishman's rapier made a silver line in the moonlight.

Far away came the mutter of the drums. Kane mechanically cleansed his sword on his tattered garments. The trail ended here, and Kane was conscious of a strange feeling of futility. He always felt that, after he had killed a foe. Somehow it always seemed that no real good had been wrought; as if the foe had, after all, escaped his just vengeance.

With a shrug of his shoulders Kane turned his attention to his bodily needs. Now that the heat of battle had passed, he began to feel weak and faint from the loss of blood. That last thrust had been close; had he not managed to avoid its full point by a twist of his body, the blade had transfixed him. As it was, the sword had struck glancingly, plowed along his ribs and sunk deep in the muscles beneath the shoulder-blade, inflicting a long, shallow wound.

Kane looked about him and saw that a small stream trickled through the glade at the far side. Here he made the only mistake of that kind that he ever made in his entire life. Mayhap he was dizzy from loss of blood and still mazed from the weird happenings of the night; be that as it may, he laid down his rapier and crossed, weaponless, to the stream. There he laved his wounds and bandaged them as best he could, with strips torn from his clothing.

Then he rose and was about to re-trace his steps when a motion among the trees on the side of the glade where he first entered, caught his eye. A huge figure stepped out of the jungle, and Kane saw, and recognized, his doom. The man was Gulka, the gorilla-slayer. Kane remembered that he had not seen the black among those doing homage to N'Longa. How could he know the craft and hatred in that dusky, slanting skull that had led the negro, escaping the vengeance of his tribesmen, to trail down the only man he had ever feared? The Black God had been kind to his neophyte; had led him upon his victim helpless and unarmed. Now Gulka could kill his man openly—and slowly, as a leopard kills, not smiting him down from ambush as he had planned, silently and suddenly.

A wide grin split the negro's face, and he moistened his lips. Kane, watching him, was coldly and deliberately weighing his chances. Gulka had already spied the rapiers. He was closer to them than was Kane. The Englishman knew that there was no chance of his winning in a sudden race for the swords.

A slow, deadly rage surged in him—the fury of helplessness. The blood churned in his temples and his eyes smoldered with a terrible light as he eyed the negro. His fingers spread and closed like claws. They were strong, those hands; men had died in their clutch. Even Gulka's huge black column of a neck might break like a rotten branch between them—a wave of weakness made the futility of these thoughts apparent to an extent that needed not the verification of the moonlight glimmering from the spear in Gulka's black hand. Kane could not even have fled had he wished—and he had never fled from a single foe.

The gorilla-slayer moved out into the glade. Massive, terrible, he was the personification of the primitive, the Stone Age. His mouth yawned in a red cavern of a grin; he bore himself with the haughty arrogance of savage might.

Kane tensed himself for the struggle that could end but one way. He strove to rally his waning forces. Useless; he had lost too much blood. At least he would meet his death on his feet, and somehow he stiffened his buckling knees and held himself erect, though the glade shimmered before him in uncertain waves and the moonlight seemed to have become a red fog through which he dimly glimpsed the approaching black man.

Kane stooped, though the effort nearly pitched him on his face; he dipped water in his cupped hands and dashed it into his face. This revived him, and he straightened, hoping that Gulka would charge and get it over with before his weakness crumpled him to the earth.

Gulka was now about the center of the glade, moving with the slow, easy stride of a great cat stalking a victim. He was not at all in a hurry to consummate his purpose. He wanted to toy with his victim, to see fear come into those grim eyes which had looked him down, even when the possessor of those eyes had been bound to the death stake. He wanted to slay, at last, slowly, glutting his tigerish blood-lust and torture-lust to the fullest extent.

Then suddenly he halted, turned swiftly, facing another side of the glade. Kane, wondering, followed his glance.

At first it seemed like a blacker shadow among the jungle shadows. At first there was no motion, no sound, but Kane instinctively knew that some terrible menace lurked there in the darkness that masked and merged the silent trees. A sullen horror brooded there, and Kane felt as if, from that monstrous shadow, inhuman eyes seared his very soul. Yet simultaneously there came the fantastic sensation that these eyes were not directed on him. He looked at the gorilla-slayer.

The black man had apparently forgotten him; he stood, half crouching, spear lifted, eyes fixed upon that clump of blackness. Kane looked again. Now there was motion in the shadows; they merged fantastically and moved out into the glade, much as Gulka had done. Kane blinked: was this the illusion that precedes death? The shape he looked upon was such as he had visioned dimly in wild nightmares, when the wings of sleep bore him back through lost ages.

He thought at first it was some blasphemous mockery of a man, for it went erect and was tall as a tall man. But it was inhumanly broad and thick, and its gigantic arms hung nearly to its misshapen feet. Then the moonlight smote full upon its bestial face, and Kane's mazed mind thought that the thing was the Black God coming out of the shadows, animated and blood-lusting. Then he saw that it was covered with hair, and he remembered the manlike thing dangling from the roof-pole in the native village. He looked at Gulka.

The negro was facing the gorilla, spear at the charge. He was not afraid, but his sluggish mind was wondering over the miracle that brought this beast so far from his native jungles.

The mighty ape came out into the moonlight and there was a terrible majesty about his movements. He was nearer Kane than Gulka but he did not seem to be aware of the white man. His small, blazing eyes were fixed on the black man with terrible intensity. He advanced with a curious swaying stride.

Far away the drums whispered through the night, like an accompaniment to this grim Stone Age drama. The savage crouched in the middle of the glade, but the primordial came out of the jungle with eyes bloodshot and blood-lusting. The negro was face to face with a thing more primitive than he. Again ghosts of memories whispered to Kane: you have seen such sights before (they murmured), back in the dim days, the dawn days, when beast and beast-man battled for supremacy.

Gulka moved away from the ape in a half-circle, crouching, spear ready. With all his craft he was seeking to trick the gorilla, to make a swift kill, for he had never before met such a monster as this, and though he did not fear, he had begun to doubt. The ape made no attempt to stalk or circle; he strode straight forward toward Gulka.

The black man who faced him and the white man who watched could not know the brutish love, the brutish hate that had driven the monster down from the low, forest-covered hills of the north to follow for leagues the trail of him who was the scourge of his kind—the slayer of his mate, whose body now hung from the roof-pole of the negro village.

The end came swiftly, almost like a sudden gesture. They were close, now, beast and beast-man; and suddenly, with an earth-shaking roar, the gorilla charged. A great hairy arm smote aside the thrusting spear, and the ape closed with the negro. There was a shattering sound as of many branches breaking simultaneously, and

Gulka slumped silently to the earth, to lie with arms, legs and body flung in strange, unnatural positions. The ape towered an instant above him, like a statue of the primordial triumphant.

Far away Kane heard the drums murmur. The soul of the jungle, the soul of the jungle: this phrase surged through his mind with monotonous reiteration.

The three who had stood in power before the Black God that night, where were they? Back in the village where the drums rustled lay Songa—King Songa, once lord of life and death, now a shriveled corpse with a face set in a mask of horror. Stretched on his back in the middle of the glade lay he whom Kane had followed many a league by land and sea. And Gulka the gorilla-slayer lay at the feet of his killer, broken at last by the savagery which had made him a true son of this grim land which had at last overwhelmed him.

Yet the Black God still reigned, thought Kane dizzily, brooding back in the shadows of this dark country, bestial, blood-lusting, caring naught who lived or died, so that he drank.

Kane watched the mighty ape, wondering how long it would be before the huge simian spied and charged him. But the gorilla gave no evidence of having even seen him. Some dim impulse of vengeance yet unglutted prompting him, he bent and raised the negro. Then he slouched toward the jungle, Gulka's limbs trailing limply and grotesquely. As he reached the trees, the ape halted, whirling the giant form high in the air with seemingly no effort, and dashed the dead man up among the branches. There was a rending sound as a broken projecting limb tore through the body hurled so powerfully against it, and the dead gorilla-slayer dangled there hideously.

A moment the clear moon limned the great ape in its glimmer, as he stood silently gazing up at his victim; then like a dark shadow he melted noiselessly into the jungle.

Kane walked slowly to the middle of the glade and took up his rapier. The blood had ceased to flow from his wounds, and some of his strength was returning, enough, at least, for him to reach the coast where his ship awaited him. He halted at the edge of the glade for a backward glance at Le Loup's upturned face and still form, white in the moonlight, and at the dark shadow among the trees that was Gulka, left by some bestial whim, hanging as the she-gorilla hung in the village.

Afar the drums muttered: "The wisdom of our land is ancient; the wisdom of our land is dark; whom we serve, we destroy. Flee if you would live, but you will never forget our chant. Never, never," sang the drums.

Kane turned to the trail which led to the beach and the ship waiting there.

THE END

NIGHT-GAUNTS

Out of what crypt they crawl, I cannot tell,
But every night I see the rubbery things,
Black, horned, and slender, with membranous wings,
They come in legions on the north wind's swell
With obscene clutch that titillates and stings,
Snatching me off on monstrous voyagings
To grey worlds hidden deep in nightmare's well.

Over the jagged peaks of Thok they sweep,
Heedless of all the cries I try to make,
And down the nether pits to that foul lake
Where the puffed shoggoths splash in doubtful sleep.
But ho! If only they would make some sound,
Or wear a face where faces should be found!

— H. P. Lovecraft
December 1939

CONTRIBUTORS

E. M. FORSTER (1879 – 1970) was an English author, best known for his novels, particularly *A Room with a View*, *Howards End*, and *A Passage to India*.

GARDNER FOX (1911 – 1986) was an American writer known best for creating numerous comic book characters for DC Comics. He is estimated to have written more than 4,000 comics stories,[4] including 1,500 for DC Comics. Fox was also a science fiction author and wrote many novels and short stories.

JOHN GRAVES publishes Literary Outlaw magazine and hosts the Literary Outlaw podcast. He lives on a working farm in the shadow of the Blue Ridge Mountains in Virginia. He's half southern, half yankee, and all American. He describes himself as an Ecclesiastes 1:17 man married to a Proverbs 31 woman. John is the author of the *Starship Gilead* trilogy and the forthcoming weird western series *Rook: God's Gunslinger*.

ROBERT E. HOWARD (1906 – 1936) was an American writer who wrote pulp fiction in a diverse range of genres. He created the character Conan the Barbarian and is regarded as the father of the sword and sorcery subgenre.

H. P. LOVECRAFT (1890 – 1937) was an American writer of weird, science, fantasy, and horror fiction. He is best known for his creation of the Cthulhu Mythos.

BOOTH TARKINGTON (1869 – 1946) was an American novelist and dramatist best known for his novels The Magnificent Ambersons (1918) and Alice Adams (1921). He is one of only four novelists to win the Pulitzer Prize for Fiction more than once.

THORNTON WILDER (1897 – 1975) was an American playwright and novelist. He won three Pulitzer Prizes for the novel *The Bridge of San Luis Rey* and for the plays *Our Town* and *The Skin of Our Teeth*.